"Lovemaking is something entirely different."

Jana looked up at him then. He lowered his head, but didn't kiss her. Instead, he touched his cheek to hers, nuzzling her, brushing his lips against her.

His mouth played along the curve of her jaw. "If you've forgotten the difference between the two," Brandon murmured against her ear, "I'll be happy to demonstrate."

His lips claimed her neck once more, sending a rush through her. Jana closed her eyes for a moment, then drew in a breath and pushed away.

"No," she said, wanting to sound forceful but failing miserably.

Brandon didn't protest, but she saw the wanting in his darkened eyes, his heavy breaths, his flushed cheeks. For an instant Jana wanted to throw herself into his arms once more, have him carry her into her bedroom as he used to do.

But that would only complicate things…!

* * *

The One Month Marriage
Harlequin Historical #726—October 2004

Praise for Judith Stacy's recent titles

"Wild West Wager" in A Hero's Kiss
"A starchy heroine and disreputable hero strike a
'Wild West Wager' that sets tongues a-wagging
in Stacy's romantic, funny tale."
—*Romantic Times*

The Nanny
"One of the most entertaining and sweetly
satisfying tales I've had the pleasure to encounter."
—*The Romance Reader*

The Blushing Bride
"...lovable characters that grab your heartstrings...
a fun read all the way."
—*Rendezvous*

The Dreammaker
"...a delightful story of the triumph of love."
—*Rendezvous*

JUDITH STACY

The One Month Marriage

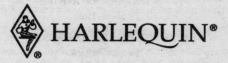

HARLEQUIN®

TORONTO • NEW YORK • LONDON
AMSTERDAM • PARIS • SYDNEY • HAMBURG
STOCKHOLM • ATHENS • TOKYO • MILAN • MADRID
PRAGUE • WARSAW • BUDAPEST • AUCKLAND

ISBN 0-373-29326-7

THE ONE MONTH MARRIAGE

Copyright © 2004 by Dorothy Howell

Please address questions and book requests to:
Harlequin Reader Service
U.S.: 3010 Walden Ave., P.O. Box 1325, Buffalo, NY 14269
Canadian: P.O. Box 609, Fort Erie, Ont. L2A 5X3

Thanks to David, Judy and Stacy
for always doing more than you have to.

And thanks to Jolene,
for being that once-in-a-lifetime friend.

Acknowledgment:

The author wishes to thank Martha Cooper
for her assistance with this book.

Chapter One

Los Angeles, 1897

So she was coming home.

Brandon Sayer stared down at the telegram lying atop the papers and ledgers on his desk. Jana was coming home. His bride—if one could be called such after so long a time—was returning.

Brandon rose from his chair and crossed to the window, his footsteps silent on the thick carpet. He gazed down at the corner of Broadway and Third, the most prestigious business address in the city of Los Angeles. The trolley, delivery wagons, private coaches and eight-team oil wagons choked the intersection. Pedestrians scurried across the street, rightly fearing for their lives. Brandon pressed his palm against the warm glass of the windowpane.

Jana was coming home.

After all this time.

"Brandon?"

He turned from the window, saw Noah Carmichael standing just inside the doorway, and suspected that Noah had called his name several times. Beyond, the sound of clicking typewriter keys and muted voices drifted in through the open door as Brandon's office staff went about their work.

"Another brilliant idea cooking in that brain of yours?" Noah asked with the easy smile their years of friendship and many successful business ventures had brought.

Brandon didn't answer. He didn't know what to say. An odd feeling for the man who, in the last five years, had built a business empire that rivaled the greatest industrialists on either coast.

Noah's eyebrows pulled together and he tossed aside the stack of papers he'd brought into the office with him.

"What's wrong?" he asked.

Brandon just stared at him for a moment, then gestured lamely at his desk. Noah picked up the telegram, read it once, twice, then let it drop.

"She's coming back?" Noah shook his head. "My God, how long has it been?"

"I'm not sure," Brandon said. But he knew. He knew exactly.

"What are you going to do?" Noah asked.

Brandon shrugged. "Do? Why would I do anything?"

"She's been gone all this time without a word—not a single word—and suddenly she's returning? You have to do *something*."

"She's my wife."

"Barely."

Brandon turned toward the window again. He couldn't argue with Noah. Everything he said was true.

After three months of marriage, Jana had left. Simply packed her belongings and disappeared. No warning, no notice, no explanation. He heard from her only once in a telegram a few days after her abrupt departure. She'd gone home to her aunt in San Francisco. They were leaving for Europe to visit a cousin.

And now she was coming home.

Brandon's stomach tightened with anticipation.

His wife was coming home. After one year, two months and six days, she was coming home.

Thank God.

"I think we're all settled now," Jana Sayer reported as she entered the parlor of the hotel suite and gestured behind her at the hallway that led to the bedrooms.

Her aunt, Maureen Armstrong, reclined on the chaise. Tall, her dark hair showing only a hint of gray, Maureen possessed a gentle, artistic soul. She preferred her own company to that of most everyone else.

"Everything's unpacked," Jana said. She'd taken care of the important matters herself, then supervised the staff of servants who'd accompanied them on their transatlantic and transcontinental journeys.

"Should we order supper?" Maureen asked, looking up from the newspaper on her lap.

Jana tucked a lock of dark hair behind her ear and sank into the wingback chair by the window. A heavy sigh slipped from her lips. The trip had been arduous, the day was late and she was tired.

"Nothing for me," Jana said.

Outside, the Los Angeles rooftops darkened in the fading light. The Morgan Hotel was among the best in the city. This suite, with its lavish maroon-and-ivory decor, marble, etched glass and silk linens was its finest.

"Perhaps I'll order a little something for myself," Maureen mused. A moment passed before she spoke again, changing the subject. "Is it tomorrow, then?"

Jana's heart fluttered, charging her with an unexpected surge of emotion, or energy—or something. She forced it down and drew in a calming breath.

"Yes, tomorrow," she said. "I'm going tomorrow."

"So soon? You're sure you'll be up to it?" Maureen asked in the kindly fashion of hers that always reminded Jana of brief childhood sicknesses or rainy days when her aunt stayed at her side, seemingly reading her thoughts and always making her feel better.

Maureen Armstrong had been doing just that for the past sixteen years since Jana's parents had been killed when she was five. Never married, Maureen had raised Jana in her San Francisco mansion as her own, long-awaited child. Both had flourished in the arrangement.

"I want to handle it right away." Jana rose from the

chair and walked closer to the window. "I want to get it over with."

Maureen folded her hands in her lap. "He'll be angry," she said softly.

The first three hellish months of her marriage flashed in Jana's mind. Whatever Brandon's feelings might be tomorrow weren't her primary concern.

Really, she didn't know what to expect from him—because he'd never expressed any emotion whatsoever about her departure. She'd received only one telegram from him, and that had been sent to Aunt Maureen shortly after Jana's departure, asking if Jana had gone home. She'd gotten nothing else from her husband. Nothing. Until three months ago. Then a letter arrived at their London town house telling—not asking—her to come home.

So here she was.

"I know it will be difficult for you to break the news," Maureen said.

Jana turned, a knot of determination tightening around her heart. "What news? I have no news for Brandon."

"No news?" Maureen frowned. "But surely you're going to tell him—"

"No."

"Jana, you can't allow him to believe—" Maureen paused. "When we were in Europe all these months, I understood why you didn't…tell him. But now that we're here?"

"He doesn't need to know."

"Then why did you agree to come here?" Maureen asked.

Jana drew in a breath. "To tell Brandon that I want a divorce."

Chapter Two

Home.

Or so she'd believed.

Jana gazed out the window of the hansom cab as it turned onto West Adams Boulevard, the place that had been her home for three months. The first time she'd laid eyes on this neighborhood of wide streets, swaying palms, wrought-iron and stone fences that fronted extravagant mansions, she'd been married but two days, and her husband had been at her side.

Fourteen months ago.

A lifetime ago.

He had built the house for her. Without really wanting to, Jana smiled as she recalled the day Brandon had told her that his wedding gift to her would be a new home in the prestigious West Adams District of Los Angeles. She'd been absolutely thrilled. But everything about Brandon was thrilling…back then.

Handsome, wealthy, successful, Brandon Sayer had instantly become the talk of the San Francisco social scene when he'd come to the city on business and been introduced into polite society. All the young women had vied for his attention. Mothers had sized him up as husband material for their daughters. Fathers had known of his business successes and wanted a part of it.

But Brandon had had eyes for only one young woman.

Jana shifted on the carriage seat, the leather creaking beneath her, as she recalled Aunt Maureen's pleasure that Brandon had asked if he could call on her. Never leaving anything to chance—especially where Jana was concerned—her aunt had paid a private investigator to delve into the past of the man who seemed too good to be true.

But Maureen's concern had been for naught. Brandon Sayer, the grandson of one of the East's wealthiest, most highly regarded industrialists, had come West to expand the family fortune in California. His parents long dead, no siblings, Brandon had forged a name in his own right and built an enviable empire for himself in Los Angeles. When he had asked for Jana's hand in marriage after a whirlwind courtship, Maureen had readily agreed.

Even now, Jana could hardly remember the details, it had all happened so quickly. Brandon had returned to Los Angeles to run his business, but had visited San Francisco as often as possible. Their long-distance courtship had continued as wedding preparations were underway. Aunt Maureen had staged the grand wedding she always dreamed of for Jana. Jana had felt as if she were a princess as she'd walked down the aisle and become Brandon's wife.

From fairy-tale bride to crying alone in her bed at night.

The hansom cab swung into the driveway and pulled to a stop, yet Jana made no move to exit. She leaned closer to the window and eyed the magnificent house that had once been her home.

Three stories tall, built entirely of redwood with brownstone trim, the mansion featured a steep roof, a grand entryway and a tower room on the front corner, all snuggled comfortably amid two lavish acres of palms, shrubs, manicured lawns and refreshing fountains. Swedish wood sculptors had hand-carved the home's woodwork, both inside and out. Italian marble and French stained glass graced the floors and windows, along with bronze hardware in all the fixtures. Brandon had spared no expense.

A lump of emotion rose in Jana's throat. How could a life that had begun with such promise have turned into…this?

For an instant, she considered shouting to the driver to take her back to the Morgan Hotel. Perhaps Aunt Maureen would come back with her when she faced Brandon? Maybe she could simply send him a letter advising him of her intentions? Or leave the whole ugly mess in the hands of her aunt's attorneys to sort through and resolve?

Jana reined in her runaway thoughts. No, she'd do none of those things. She'd face Brandon. After all, she was hardly the same woman she'd been when she married him. Many things had changed these past fourteen months—none more than Jana herself.

With a quick, determined breath, she allowed the driver to assist her from the cab.

"Please wait," she said, passing him the fare and a generous tip. "I won't be long."

After all, how long could it take to advise one's husband of an impending divorce?

"Thank you, ma'am," the driver said, tipping his hat and stepping out of her way.

Jana squared her shoulders and climbed the steps to the double front doors. She stopped, unsure of what to do. Knock, or simply walk inside? Neither seemed quite right.

But she was saved from the dilemma when the door opened in front of her.

Brandon?

Jana's heart slammed against her chest and rose into her throat. Did she look all right? She'd chosen to wear for the occasion a dark blue skirt, drawn across her front and gathered high in a bustle, a matching jacket with leg-o-mutton sleeves, an ivory blouse closed at the throat with a large bow. Her wide-brimmed hat dipped fashionably over one eye.

Had the ride over crushed her skirt? Was her hat on straight? Would Brandon like the dress she'd selected, notice the darker color or the—?

"Ah, Mrs. Sayer." Charles, the white-haired butler stood in the open doorway, giving Jana the closest thing to a smile she'd ever seen on the man's face.

"Hello, Charles," she replied, chastising herself for her runaway thoughts a moment ago.

"Welcome home," he said, stepping back and gesturing her into the house.

For a moment she hesitated. Home? This wasn't her home. It had never been her home. Her home was in San Francisco with her aunt, not here—

Jana pushed the thought aside, gathered her skirt and stepped into the vestibule.

The red marble foyer, the sweeping staircase, the woodwork, the stained glass, the sights, the smells…the memories. The assault on her senses stopped Jana still in her tracks.

Over the past fourteen months, she'd occasionally wondered if the three months of her marriage had really happened. Had it instead been just a dream—a bad dream?

No. It had been real. Every moment of it. The memories twisted Jana's stomach, as painful and strong as the actual experiences had been all those months ago.

She steeled herself, pushing away the hurtful thoughts. She had to be strong. She *would* be strong. After all, she wasn't in this alone.

A warm shudder swept over her, prickling her skin and standing the hair at her nape on end.

Brandon.

She turned and saw him striding toward her. Her

knees weakened and her heart thumped wildly beneath her breast.

Good gracious, he was handsome. Tall, broad-shouldered, brown hair highlighted with the gold of the California sun, piercing blue eyes.

He'd grown even more good-looking these past fourteen months. How could that be possible?

And how could she still sense his presence after all this time?

For an instant, the need to run to him overwhelmed Jana. She wanted to snuggle against his hard chest, feel his arms pull her close.

But Brandon stopped at the edge of the foyer, as if some unseen line had been drawn between them and he wouldn't step over it. His face was set in hard, cautious lines, a look Jana had seen far too many times already.

Her surge of emotion—or whatever it was—ebbed. Jana reminded herself why she was here…and why she'd left in the first place.

A long, tense moment dragged by with them eyeing each other from opposite ends of the foyer. What do a husband and wife say after so much time apart? Jana decided to leave that up to Brandon. It was he, after all, who'd asked her to come home.

"You're looking well," Brandon said.

His voice sent a tremor down her spine, bringing with it the memory of the first time she'd heard his voice. Standing in a friend's parlor she'd been swathed in pale pink. Brandon, tall and sturdy among the delicate fur-

nishings, had looked so handsome she hadn't thought
she could manage to speak a single word, and then—

Again, Jana pushed aside the memory and replied,
"You're looking well also."

Her tone matched his, so they both sounded as if
they'd just encountered a casual acquaintance whose
name neither could remember.

"How was your crossing?" Brandon asked.

"Calm."

"And the rail journey?"

"Uneventful."

"Is your aunt well?"

"In excellent health, thank you," Jana replied.

Conversation stalled, but the awkward moment continued. Jana hadn't really expected her husband to
sweep her into his arms, profess his love, pour out his
regret and apology, but she'd seen Brandon give warmer
receptions to business acquaintances.

"Perhaps we should go into my office?" he asked,
gesturing behind him.

There was no reason not to. After all, they could hardly
discuss their situation standing in the foyer. Charles had
disappeared, as butlers always do, but she was certain he
and some of the other staff were well within earshot. Yet
going deeper into the house—with Brandon—caused
Jana's palms to dampen and set her nerves on end.

The heat of his body wafted over her as she crossed
the foyer and he fell in step beside her. His scent came
with the heat, stirring her memories once more.

As they passed the parlor doorway, Jana glanced inside, then stopped and gasped aloud. The room that she'd begun decorating—along with the entire rest of the house—stood just as she'd left it fourteen months ago. One wall half papered, cans of paint in the corner, shrouded furniture pushed to the center of the room.

"You never finished the work?" she asked, unable to keep the surprise from her voice.

"No, of course not," Brandon replied, as if he didn't really understand why she would ask such a question.

He continued down the hallway leaving her to follow. When she stepped into Brandon's office, another wave of emotion struck her. The room, with its heavy walnut furniture, deep green carpet and drapes, had been the first completed in the new house. The decorator—that dreadful Mr. McDowell—had seen to it. No one had asked Jana's opinion of the color scheme or the furnishings. Or anything else, for that matter.

But it suited Brandon. The office was his refuge. He spent most of his time there, when he was home. Jana had seldom entered the room.

How odd that she'd be there today, when she intended to end their marriage.

Somehow, she couldn't bring herself to sit on the dark leather sofa. She stood, with the oil painting of cornered foxes, snarling bears and mountain lions glaring down at her.

"I see you've kept everything here the same," she couldn't help but say.

Brandon's gaze bounced from wall to wall, then fell on her again as she stood a few yards in front of him.

"Why would I change it?" he asked, frowning slightly.

Why, indeed? Brandon preferred—demanded—things stay the same. Jana knew that all too well.

A long silence passed, and finally Brandon spoke again.

"So," he said briskly. "You're home now. That's the important thing. We can put all this nonsense behind us and—"

"Nonsense?"

"Yes," he went on, rubbing his palms together. "We can forget about what you did, and get on with our lives."

Stunned, Jana just stared, unable to speak.

Brandon moved to his desk and began sorting through papers. "You'll want to continue with decorating the house and pick up where you left off with the women's organizations in town. The servants have done an adequate job, but you'll need to supervise them more closely this time. There are invitations and correspondence that you will need to attend to before—"

"You…you expect me to take over all my old duties?" Jana asked, shaking her head slowly. "Is that why you think I came back?"

Brandon's hands stilled on the papers and his gaze came up quickly. "Well, yes."

"That's not why I came here," Jana said. "I'm only here to tell you I want a divorce."

Breath left Brandon in a huff as color drained from his face. Jana rushed on, anxious to get this ordeal over with, to leave and never return.

"My aunt's attorneys will arrange everything," she said. Brandon didn't respond.

"You needn't worry. I won't ask for anything." Jana gestured around the room. "You can keep it all."

"No..."

"I'll be certain everything is handled quickly. Goodbye, Brandon," she said, and hurried toward the door.

"No!"

The wrath, the raw anger in Brandon's voice brought Jana up short. She whirled. Fists clenched, shoulders rigid, jaw set, Brandon glared at her.

She hadn't expected him to say nothing at all. But she hadn't expected him to disagree, either. After all, it had been fourteen months, fourteen long months, with no communication whatsoever. Certainly, Jana hadn't anticipated the fury she saw now on her husband's face.

He came around the desk. "You want a—a—a *divorce?*"

Jana drew up her courage. "Yes."

Brandon didn't speak, just glared. She rushed on, feeling pressured to explain. "I've been gone too long. We're practically strangers."

"No..."

Jana drew in a breath. "Our marriage is dead."

"No!"

She dug deep, finding the calm she'd struggled to develop these last fourteen months. "Brandon, you have to face the truth. It's over."

"We're married," Brandon told her, his anger growing. "Whether you like it or not. Legally and in the eyes of God. We're married."

Her anger flared. "I hardly need you to remind me of the vows I took."

"Somebody needs to." Brandon flung the words at her. "Before you go running off again."

"I don't deserve to be spoken to as if—"

"And fourteen months ago I deserved to hear you tell me to my face that you were leaving!"

"I was gone *two days* before you realized I'd left!"

That shut him up. Brandon's anger subsided, but only a little. He drew in a breath and tilted his head left, then right, easing the tension in his neck, as she'd seen him do so many times before.

"At the time, I was heavily involved in a crucial business deal that was teetering on collapse, if you recall," Brandon explained, his voice softer but just as tense. "I had early-morning meetings, meetings that stretched into the night. It didn't occur to me to look into my wife's bedroom each evening to see whether or not she'd run off."

Jana met his gaze but didn't answer. His explanation was reasonable, yet didn't erase the pain she'd gone through at the time.

After another long moment, Brandon spoke again, his voice straining for calm.

"As I said, we are married. You and I are bound together by law and in the sight of God. Our marriage isn't over simply because you declare it to be."

A thread of panic whipped through Jana. "We haven't seen each other in months. We hardly knew each other to begin with—"

"Then how can you know that our marriage is over?" Brandon demanded, his eyes boring into her. "How can you declare it dead when we haven't even given it a fair chance?"

Jana determinedly held herself rigid, refusing to let him see the chaos his words—his logic—stirred in her.

"What makes you think, after all this time and all that's happened, that we can make it work?" Jana demanded.

"Nothing's happened that can't be undone," Brandon insisted.

Jana gulped, guilt replacing her panic. "That's not true. Things—"

He put up his hand, silencing her. "Perhaps we can't work out these problems you believe we have. But we won't know unless we try."

Her resolve crumbled further. "Brandon, it's not that simple."

"Yes, it is," he said. "And if our marriage dies, at least it will die with us trying to do the right thing."

Jana's knees weakened, but for a different reason now. Never—ever—had she imagined Brandon would be so adamant about keeping their marriage together. She had no idea their union meant so much, or anything at all, to him.

"Just say you'll try," Brandon said.

Did she hear a plea in his voice? She wasn't sure.

Jana shook her head. "I can't live here forever, waiting, wondering how things will turn out."

"Then give it a month," Brandon said quickly. "Four weeks. Our vows are worth that much, aren't they?"

Jana didn't reply. How could she disagree?

"I'll think it over," she finally said.

That didn't seem to suit him, but he nodded. "Tomorrow? You'll give me your answer?"

"Yes, I'll come back tomorrow. Before six," Jana said, the old habit returning without her even realizing it. Six o'clock. He had always wanted her home before six o'clock.

"Promise?"

An odd wave of vulnerability sounded in his voice, and for an instant, he looked hurt and lost, touching Jana's heart unexpectedly, making her want to rush to him, touch her palm to his cheek, soothe him.

But in the next instant, Brandon's expression hardened again and so did Jana's heart.

"I'll be here before six o'clock," she told him. "I promise."

Brandon just nodded. He stood there looking at her for a while, and Jana didn't know what to do or say. Nothing seemed appropriate, so she simply turned and left. To her surprise, Brandon walked alongside her through the house and out into the driveway. He waved off the driver up top and opened the hansom door for her himself. .

"I'll send my carriage for you tomorrow," Brandon said.

"It's not necessary."

He gestured to the cab. "You needn't ride around in public transportation. I'll send my carriage—"

Jana touched his arm, even though she hadn't meant to.

"I said I'll be here tomorrow, and I will," she told him.

His jaw tightened, but finally he nodded. "Fine, then."

Jana climbed into the cab, pointedly ignoring his proffered hand. Brandon closed the door and held on to the handle.

He gazed at her though the open window. "There must have been something…something you liked about our marriage."

"No."

"Something you liked about…us."

Jana gazed steadily at him. "Nothing."

Brandon stepped back and signaled the driver who turned the cab into the street. Jana watched out the window at Brandon standing on the steps, following the cab with his gaze.

She turned away, slumping deeper into the seat.

How could she live here, in the house, for four weeks? How could she manage it…when her heart was somewhere else?

Chapter Three

~~~~~~~~~~~~~~~~~~~~~~

Raised voices in the outer office took Brandon's attention from the ledger that lay open on his desk. Glad for the distraction, he closed the book. He couldn't concentrate on the figures anyway.

How could he after last night?

The commotion beyond his closed office door continued. Brandon heard the voice of his secretary, Mr. Perkins, raised in protest. Still, Brandon remained in his chair, confident the white-haired, wiry secretary could handle whatever situation presented itself.

Brandon had no energy for confrontation today. Since receiving the telegram from Jana advising him of her return, he'd slept little. All he could think was that, at last, the ordeal would be over. His wife was returning. He'd thought everything would be back to normal.

Brandon sank lower in his chair, tuning out the dis-

turbance in the outer office, preferring thoughts of
his wife.

Their fourteen-month separation had changed her in
subtle ways. He noticed each and every one of them yesterday when they'd stood across the foyer from each other
and he'd been trying to put together a cohesive sentence.

Even more beautiful. The notion had hit him square
in the chest yesterday. Her face a little more mature, after
so short a time, her dress more sophisticated, her figure
a trifle fuller. He had wanted her right there in the foyer.

He had wanted her even when she asked for a divorce.

Brandon grumbled aloud. A divorce. What nonsense.
True, Jana had been young, pampered and spoiled when
they married. She'd run back home to her aunt who,
with the best of intentions, had taken her in and allowed
Jana to accompany her on a long-planned extended trip
to Europe. Brandon understood how impetuous his
young wife had been, and how her aunt couldn't say no.
He'd indulged them both.

But now—

His office door burst open and Mr. Perkins rushed
into the room on the heels of the woman who had,
surely, been the cause of the commotion.

"Now see here, madam," Mr. Perkins barked, his
face red. "You can't come pushing your way in here. I
told you that Mr. Sayer isn't seeing anyone today without an appointment, and you haven't—"

"Since when do I need an appointment?"

Leona Albright directed her question at Brandon,

her words a seductive whisper that brought him out of his chair.

Seeing his battle lost, Mr. Perkins turned to Brandon. "I told her, Mr. Sayer, I told her you weren't seeing anyone today without an appointment. That those were your instructions and I couldn't allow—"

"It's all right," Brandon said.

"I told that young fella from the newspaper the same thing this morning. That Mr. Fisk. I told him you weren't seeing anyone today without an appointment." Mr. Perkins threw Leona Albright a scathing look. "Only *he* had the decency to respect your wishes and go about his business."

"Thank you, Mr. Perkins," Brandon said. "I'll speak with Mrs. Albright."

Mr. Perkins shot her a final contemptuous glare, then huffed out of the office, closing the door with a little more force than necessary.

Leona, her gaze still on Brandon, gave him a slow, steady smile, one that brought lesser men to their knees.

"You've been keeping secrets, Brandon, dear," she purred and walked closer.

"You like secrets," he countered.

Leona Albright did indeed like secrets. She liked everything. Tall, ten years older than Brandon, though she'd never admit it to anyone else, Leona wore her dresses cut a fraction lower than was considered decent—especially for her ample figure—and her hair a shade more fiery red than nature alone could provide.

Yet her wealth, her social position and political connections on both coasts kept anyone from commenting—in public, anyway. She'd recently lost her fourth, much-older husband and, according to the latest rumor, had already turned down two marriage proposals.

"You know me well," Leona purred.

"Which of my secrets have you uncovered?" he asked, motioning her toward the seating group at the other end of his office.

Leona took her time settling onto the sofa, arranging her skirt, shifting her shoulders in a way that called attention to her impressive bosom. Brandon took the chair to her immediate left.

"I'm terribly hurt," Leona declared. "This Jennings deal of yours. You never mentioned a word of it to me."

"There's talk?" Brandon asked, a little concerned.

"Whispers," Leona said, and raised an eyebrow suggestively. "I learned of it from an unnamed, but very satisfied, source."

The Jennings Building, a five-story structure in a prime location, currently housed the *Los Angeles Messenger.* Brandon owned both the newspaper and the building. Over the last year he'd refused to renew the leases of tenants until now only the newspaper remained. It, too, would be gone soon. Then his new project would be officially announced, though it had been quietly in the works for some time.

"And is this 'unnamed source' of yours interested in the project?" Brandon asked.

"Of course," Leona said. "Everyone is interested in anything that involves you, Brandon, dear. Your name attached to any project guarantees success."

Brandon smiled, not unhappy to hear a compliment.

"All right," he said. "I'll give you the details before the public announcement."

"Of course you will," Leona said, favoring him with another smile. "Now, on to your next secret."

Brandon frowned, trying to imagine what she referred to this time.

"The return of your wife," Leona said. "I admit, I'm surprised you're even here at your office today."

Brandon shifted uncomfortably on the sofa. He was certain everyone who'd heard of Jana's return was curious to find him at work today, rather than at home rolling around in bed with her, making up for their fourteen-month separation.

The playfulness left Leona's face. "Not a joyful reunion?"

"Not exactly," Brandon said. He didn't hesitate to explain further, knowing Leona would keep his confidence, even to unnamed—but satisfied—sources.

It wasn't the first time she'd kept silent on his behalf.

"She wants a divorce," Brandon explained. "I told her no, of course. She agreed to work on our marriage."

"So you have everything under control," Leona said.

Brandon nodded. He'd thought about it all last night, all morning, all afternoon. He knew what to do.

"Jana is my wife. She must live up to her responsibilities. It's her duty."

"You romantic devil, you," Leona said.

Brandon sat forward. "I have duties in our marriage.
She does too. Everyone has duties. We all must live up
to them."

"Duties?"

"Of course," Brandon said. "Jana needed a firm hand.
It was my fault she left, really. I was too easy on her. I'll
be sure she understands her responsibilities this time."

"Well, as long as you have everything under control..." Leona rose from the sofa, bringing Brandon up
with her. She gave him a long, sultry look. "You should
have married me."

"All your husbands die."

"But they go with smiles on their faces." Leona saun-
tered to the office door, threw him one last knowing
look, and left.

"I see you've made your decision," Maureen said.

Jana glanced back at her maid closing the latches on
her trunk. "It wasn't exactly *my* decision," she said. "Brandon refused to grant me a divorce unless I did as he asked."

"He has a point," Maureen said.

Jana didn't respond, just moved past her aunt, down
the hallway and into the parlor of the suite. Brandon did,
indeed, have a point. It was all she'd been able to think
about since they'd talked yesterday.

Legally and in the eyes of God they were married.

Brandon had been right about that. And Jana could find no argument to refute his assertion. She'd taken vows, pledged her life to their union. None of which should be taken lightly.

It had all seemed so much easier, so much clearer in London. There, she'd known exactly what she wanted. With the distance from her husband, she'd realized exactly what sort of man he was—and what sort of man she wanted.

But after seeing him again yesterday…

Jana sank onto the settee. She'd tossed and turned, paced the floor all night. Was she being foolish? Wishing for something that would never be there? Expecting more from Brandon than he'd given in the past?

Or had he changed? She certainly wasn't the same person she was fourteen months ago. Could Brandon have changed, as well?

For better or worse, their marriage vows had stated. Could the "worse" really be behind her?

Jana sensed her aunt come into the parlor and rose from the settee. "I owe it to the marriage to give it another chance."

Aunt Maureen raised her brows. "And you'll do that? Give it an honest chance?"

Jana nodded. She'd do just that. If not, why bother with it at all?

"I think it's better that we try one last time," Jana said. "As Brandon says, if it still doesn't work at least we'll know we tried to do the right thing."

Maureen nodded. "It will be easier to explain… later on."

Doubt swept through Jana, but she pushed on.

"You'll take care of everything here?" she asked. She'd discussed it with her aunt already and she'd agreed, but Jana felt she had to ask one last time.

"I'm ready for some rest, some solitude." Maureen gestured toward the window. "The sunsets here are glorious, at times. I want to try and capture them on canvas. I have books to read and poetry to write. I'll be fine, dear. Don't give it a thought."

"I'll come visit every day," Jana told her.

Maureen smiled gently. "I understand."

Jana took one last look around, then drew in a breath. "Well, I'd better go."

She pinned on her hat and found her handbag as the servants took her trunk out the door.

"I'll see to it the rest of your things are packed and sent over tomorrow," Maureen promised, then as if reading Jana's thoughts added, "Don't worry. I won't let any of our staff go to the house. Someone from the hotel will deliver your things."

Jana rushed to her aunt and gave her a quick hug. "If anything happens—anything at all—let me know. Day or night. Don't hesitate."

"Of course, dear," Aunt Maureen promised.

With a final hug and peck on the cheek, Jana left the suite and set off yet again for her new life with Brandon.

When she arrived at the house on West Adams, Jana

instructed the hansom driver to place her trunk on the front porch. Somehow, she couldn't bring herself to have it taken inside just yet. She wanted to talk to Brandon first, be sure they both understood their arrangement.

Parts of it he wouldn't like. She was sure of it.

And if they reached an agreement on their unorthodox arrangement, today—though only a few hours were left in it—would count as day one. Twenty-nine to go.

"Good evening, Mrs. Sayer," Charles greeted her as she stepped into the vestibule. He eyed the trunk, but didn't say anything.

"Good evening, Charles," Jana said, glancing around, expecting to see Brandon waiting. It wasn't quite six o'clock, her designated arrival time, so she was a bit early. "Would you tell him I'm here, please?"

"Mr. Sayer isn't home."

A knot jerked in Jana's stomach. "He's not here?" she asked, hearing the accusation in her voice. Though only *she* was supposed to be home by six, she expected Brandon to be here also, under the circumstances.

Charles cast his gaze away. "No, ma'am."

"I see." Jana drew herself up. "Cook is preparing supper?"

"Yes, ma'am. Seven o'clock, as always."

"Of course. Seven o'clock." How could she have forgotten Brandon's designated supper hour?

"Shall I have Cook prepare you some refreshment?" Charles asked.

"No, thank you." Jana removed her hat and passed it

to the butler along with her handbag. "That's all, Charles. Thank you."

He dipped his head slightly and crept away.

Jana moved through the still house, switching on lights as she went. The fixtures had been built for both gas and electricity. Tonight, the electrical current flowed smoothly, making the more reliable gas jets unnecessary.

In the parlor, the light cast a harsh glare on the half-papered walls and reflected off the white furniture shrouds. The smell of paint hung faintly in the air. Jana stood in the center of the room, turning to take it all in.

Good gracious, had she really picked out this wall-paper, this paint color? And the mural on the ceiling. A hunting scene? Hideous. What had she been thinking?

Her thinking had been just fine fourteen months ago, she suddenly remembered. But no one had been interested in her opinion.

The color samples, fabric and wallpaper swatches were piled in a heap on the shrouded settee. Jana sat down and immersed herself in them, her mind filling with ideas that would do this room justice. She lost track of the time until, vaguely, she heard a clock chime the hour once more. Seven o'clock.

Seven o'clock and no Brandon. Jana rose from the settee and went to the vestibule. She peeked out. Gas-lights burned on West Adams Boulevard. The trolley had stopped for the night, but carriages made their way up and down the street.

No sign of Brandon.

At seven-thirty, Jana went to the dining room, ate alone, then returned to the parlor. At eight-fifteen Brandon arrived home. She went to meet him.

"You're here. Good," he said, passing his bowler and satchel to Charles, and striding across the foyer to where she waited. He looked rushed, hurried, distracted.

"I ate supper already," Jana told him, just for something to say.

He frowned. "You know I prefer we eat together. Well, no matter—this time. I saw your trunk outside. I'm glad you've come to your senses. Have it brought inside and—"

"We need to talk first."

Brandon stopped, seemed confused for a moment, then nodded. "Well, all right."

She trailed along behind him as he strode to his office. He flipped through a stack of envelopes on his desk, then glanced up.

"So, you're staying," he said. "Good. We can—"

"For thirty days," Jana pointed out. "I'll give it a month. That's our agreement. Unless, of course, at some point you change your mind."

Brandon frowned. "I have no intention of changing my mind."

"Fourteen months have passed," Jana said. "You might realize too much is different now."

"Nothing's different," he insisted.

"It was your idea that we try again," Jana said. "If you

find that it's a mistake, I won't hold you to the agreement. I think that's only fair."

"Fine, then." Brandon went to the door, called for Charles, then instructed him to have Jana's trunk taken to her room.

When he turned to Jana again, his expression changed. It was subtle, unnoticeable to anyone who didn't know him well. Darker eyes, deeper breathing.

She knew what it meant.

"Shall we go…upstairs?" he asked, his voice low.

Jana didn't answer. He walked beside her through the hallway, up the wide curving staircase, down the carpeted corridor to the suite of rooms they'd occupied as husband and wife.

Jana opened her door and walked inside, feeling the heat of Brandon's body behind her. She hadn't delivered all her conditions for staying yet. She'd saved the last one for now because she intended to deliver it at this time and at this place, so as to leave no question in Brandon's mind.

She swung around to face him. "Where are you going?"

Brandon stopped short in the doorway. His gaze darted past her, then landed on her again, looking slightly confused.

"Your room is next door, if I recall," she said.

He frowned, as if still not understanding. "But this is your room, and here is where we always used to…you know."

"Well, there will be no 'you knowing' between us," Jana informed him.

Color drained from his face. "But…"

"Not for thirty days, anyway."

"Thirty days?"

"It's the trial period you agreed to," she reminded him.

"Yes, but I didn't think you meant we couldn't—"

"Our lives are too unsettled," Jana said. "We wouldn't want to complicate them further."

"But—I—"

"Good night, Brandon."

"But—"

She closed the door in his face.

Chapter Four

A brisk knock and the door easing open brought Jana fully awake. She pushed herself up, holding the bedcovers over her breasts, and tossed her dark hair over her shoulder.

Brandon? Her heart thumped harder, jolting her. Was Brandon entering her room? Last night she'd forbidden him to enter and he'd respected her wishes. But now at dawn, had he changed his mind?

Jana squinted across the room and blinked the sleep from her eyes, bringing into focus the figure of a young woman, not her husband, entering her bedchamber.

"Abbie? Is that you?"

"Yes, Mrs. Sayer. Good morning," the maid replied crossing to the bed.

Jana sat up, genuinely pleased by something in this house for the first time since her arrival.

"Good gracious," Jana said, "I can't believe it's really you. You're still here?"

Abbie smiled, a warm familiar smile, looking equally pleased. "Yes, ma'am. I'm still here. After all this time."

"But—how? Why? I thought you'd be long gone."

The young woman—not much older than Jana—had been her maid when she'd first arrived here as Brandon's new wife. Abbie didn't look any different, dark curls barely contained in her white cap, gray uniform with crisp apron, a pleasant smile on her face. Abbie had been Jana's lifeline, at times, during that tumultuous period.

"I thought I'd be let go for sure, after you left," Abbie confided. "But Mr. Sayer wouldn't have no part of it. He said I was to stay. For when you got back."

Jana's stomach twisted into a knot. "When I...got back?"

"Yes, ma'am," Abbie assured her, bustling about the room, picking up the clothing Jana had left on a chair last night. "I'm truly sorry, ma'am, that I wasn't here when you arrived. My aunt, she was feeling a bit under the weather, so I was visiting with her. Charles, he sent for me, told me to get back here straightaway."

"It's all right, Abbie," Jana said. "I managed well enough for myself last night."

Abbie turned to her, Jana's dress folded across her arm. "It's good to see you again, Mrs. Sayer. Truly, it is."

"Thank you, Abbie," she replied, climbing out of the bed.

"Does this mean you're staying?" she asked. "This time?"

Jana could have been insulted by Abbie's question, offended by her impertinence. But Jana liked her. They'd become more than employer and maid in the past. Jana could use Abbie's allegiance—and confidence—this time, as well.

"I wanted a divorce, but Brandon insisted we give our marriage another chance," Jana told her. "I decided we should do just that...and see what happens."

Abbie cast a pointed glance at the bed, the covers still tucked in neatly at the bottom, barely disturbed. But she said nothing as she headed for the large redwood closet.

With the first rays of morning sunlight beaming in through the heavy drapes, Jana's room brightened slowly, giving her a good look at the things she'd barely noticed last night in her haste to get into bed.

She turned in a slow circle, and stopped still in the center of the room.

Nothing had changed.

Nothing. Absolutely nothing. All stood exactly as she'd left it fourteen months ago.

The bed with the pink-and-white coverlet. The cherry furniture. Her dressing table with the carved ivory brush set, the ostrich feather perfume bottles, jars of lotion, powder and creams—all exactly where she left them.

"Mr. Sayer wouldn't let us change nothing."

Jana turned at the sound of Abbie's voice. "What?"

"Not one thing was to be moved. Everything was to

be left exactly as it was." Abbie rolled her eyes. "And when one of the girls—you remember Rita, don't you?—when she suggested everything ought to be packed away, Mr. Sayer hit the ceiling."

"Brandon became angry?" Jana asked, trying to picture it in her mind. In all their time together, courting and during the three months of their marriage, Jana had seldom heard Brandon raise his voice. She couldn't ever remember him becoming truly angry.

"Yes," Abbie declared, nodding her head. She leaned a little closer. "He fired Rita on the spot."

Jana gasped. "He didn't."

"He did." Abbie nodded once more. "And he wouldn't let your bed linens be washed, either. Not for the longest time."

Jana hardly knew what to make of this. But then, she reminded herself, much about her husband always had been a mystery.

"I'm glad you're still here, Abbie," Jana said, picking up her handbag from the bureau.

"Thank you, ma'am," Abbie said, then seeming to sense a change in Jana, stopped her work.

"You, of all people, understand the reasons I left," Jana said.

Abbie nodded. "I do. Yes."

"You were a great comfort to me during that time," Jana said. "I appreciated that."

"Yes, ma'am," Abbie replied, frowning slightly, obviously wondering where this conversation was going.

"You're employed by Brandon. Everyone here is," Jana said, waving her hand to indicate the entire house. "But I want to hire you away. I want you to work for me."

"But Mrs. Sayer, I do work for you. I'm your personal maid. Everything I do is—"

"No, you don't understand," Jana said. "You're a good person, Abbie, so I don't want you to feel your loyalties are divided. I'll pay your salary myself—confidentially, of course—to you personally. You can have it in addition to whatever Brandon pays you."

Jana pulled a wad of money from her handbag and thrust it at Abbie. The maid's eyes bulged and her mouth sagged open.

"Take it," Jana said. "Go on, take it."

"But..." Abbie accepted the bills, holding them at arm's length. "This is too much. Much too much. Mr. Sayer doesn't pay me near this amount. It's not right—"

"Yes, it is," Jana told her. "You work for me now. All I ask is that you keep this arrangement to yourself. No one is to know, not your family, friends, and certainly not the other servants."

"Yes, ma'am, if that's what you want—"

"And," Jana told her, "you are to speak to no one about what you might hear...or see...here in my room."

Abbie's expression darkened. But she nodded in agreement. "Yes, ma'am."

Jana sighed with relief. "Thank you, Abbie. Now, I need to dress so I can join Brandon for breakfast."

Abbie's brows rose. "You do?"

She nodded briskly. "I do."

The maid shrugged as if she didn't understand that either, and set about laying out Jana's clothes.

Brandon was already seated at the table, when Jana arrived in the breakfast room. The small, oval room was painted pale yellow and featured windows on two sides to let in the morning sun. The gardens just outside offered a view of blooming flowers and climbing roses.

Jana paused in the doorway, her breath suddenly catching. The view of her husband was nothing to be ignored either.

Brandon sat at the table turned out quite nicely in a dark blue suit, snowy shirt and deep red necktie. His wide shoulders and broad chest couldn't be hidden beneath the cut of the cloth. His big hand and long fingers grasped a fork as his attention shifted back and forth between the two newspapers laid out on the table beside his plate.

And why had she denied him entrance to her bedchamber last night...?

Jana quickly banished the thought and entered the breakfast room.

"Good morning," she said, a little surprised to hear the effortless cheer that lightened her voice.

Brandon's gaze jumped to her and quickly ran the length of her, head to toe. He flushed slightly, making her more than pleased with the forest-green dress she'd selected for the morning.

He rose from his chair, catching the linen napkin in his lap before it fell.

Was he glad to see her? Jana couldn't tell.

"Good morning," Brandon said, watching her carefully, cautiously almost.

A moment passed and finally Jana said, "I thought I'd join you for breakfast."

"Well…" Brandon glanced at the two newspapers on the table. "You know I always eat breakfast alone, but well, if you'd like to it's fine…this time."

He rounded the table and pulled out a chair for her at the opposite end. For a few seconds she thought he was staring at her backside as she lowered herself into the seat, then dismissed the idea. Her imagination, surely.

A maid entered the room, greeted her and poured coffee as Brandon resumed his chair and his reading.

Another long moment passed in silence after the maid disappeared. The clock in the hallway ticked.

"I see you're reading two newspapers?" Jana ventured.

Brandon looked up. "The *Times* and the *Messenger*," he said and turned back to his reading.

Jana fiddled with her spoon. "I thought it would be nice if we hosted an informal supper."

Brandon looked up again, a frown on his face. "A supper?"

"Yes, so that I can get reaquainted with—"

"You know I like the house quiet."

Jana shifted in her chair. "Yes, but since I've been away, I thought a small supper would be a good way—"

Brandon pushed out of his chair, then folded and

tucked both newspapers under his arm. "When I come home in the evenings after a busy, sometimes difficult day, I want things quiet. I don't like suppers and that sort of thing, and you know it. I don't know why you'd even suggest it."

"But—"

"I'm going to the office." Brandon stopped in the doorway. "I notified that decorator, the one who was here before, what's-his-name, that you're ready to resume work on the house."

Jana's eyes widened. "Mr. McDowell?"

"Whatever." Brandon dismissed the name with a wave of his hand. "He'll be here today."

"But—"

Brandon walked away without another word, without listening, leaving Jana with a familiar knot of dismay coiling in her stomach.

After a moment, she went up to her room, fetched her hat and handbag, and left the house. At the corner of West Adams Boulevard and St. James Place, she boarded the trolley, paid her nickel fare and spent the day with her aunt.

She was at the house again that evening, well before the designated six o'clock hour. Not that it mattered. Jana passed the time in the one and only decent sitting room until shortly after seven when she ate supper alone, her only company an occasional servant and the ticking of the hallway clock. When Brandon arrived home just after eight, Jana was on her way upstairs.

She turned on the bottom step, watching as he gave

Charles his bowler and satchel. After what must have been a long, trying day for him, Brandon still looked fresh…handsome.

Jana silently reprimanded herself for having the thought.

"I received a telephone call from Mr. McDowell today," Brandon said to her.

"And good evening to you, too," she countered.

He didn't notice. "McDowell told me he came by the house but you weren't here."

"That's correct."

"I told you he was coming by."

"I'm aware of that," Jana said. "But, Brandon, I don't like—"

"I expect things to get back to normal."

"Back to the way they were?"

"Certainly," Brandon told her.

Jana stood on the step a moment longer, gazing at him, fighting off a dozen storming emotions.

"You really have no idea at all why I left, do you," she said. It was a statement, not a question, because she knew without a doubt that he was completely ignorant on the subject.

Brandon just stood there, staring, looking confused, as if trying to understand where her comment had come from, why she'd said it.

When he came up with no response, Jana knew she'd gotten her answer after all.

She turned her back on him and climbed the stairs.

Chapter Five

Brandon slapped the papers down on his office desk. "Unacceptable."

In the chair across from him, Noah Carmichael raised an eyebrow. "Frankly, Brandon, I thought you'd be in a little better mood, now that your wife is back."

Brandon's already grumpy disposition grew more foul. He glared at Noah and sat back in his chair. Outside the open window, noise from the traffic on Third and Broadway drifted in, a low hum that was at times soothing, other times irritating.

Today it was irritating. Like everything else in Brandon's life.

"I take it your reunion isn't going exactly as you'd planned," Noah ventured.

"That's for damn sure," he grumbled. He sat up straighter in the chair. "Last night she accused me of having no idea why she left."

"And do you?"

"Of course," Brandon declared.

"You know because you asked her?"

"Well, no." Brandon shoved out of his chair. "I don't need to ask her. I already know."

Noah eased back and folded his arms over his chest. "You're even more brilliant than I suspected, Brandon, if you can know what's in a woman's mind."

"It wasn't hard to figure out," Brandon insisted, striding toward the window.

"Did you talk to her about it?"

He glanced back. "Talk to her?"

"Yes, talk. Women like to talk."

"Oh, hell…" Brandon stopped and huffed. "Since when did your six-month marriage make you an expert on women?"

"My wife is still in town," Noah pointed out gently. "And still warming my bed."

Heat slashed through Brandon at the thought—the very thought—of having Jana in bed again. Her warm, supple body. Her arms cradling him. Her legs entwined with his.

During their three months together, Jana had been receptive to their lovemaking, anxious, he'd thought, to share her bed with him. He couldn't remember one single time—not once—that she'd not happily welcomed him.

And now, after fourteen very long months of separation, she insisted that they wait *another* month? Brandon didn't understand it. Nor did he know how he'd endure it.

"You should talk to her," Noah said.

A new flash of irritation came over Brandon as he realized he was once more standing at the window, staring out. He turned away quickly, shoving away the realization and the old feelings that came with it.

"It couldn't hurt," Noah offered, rising from his chair.

He didn't disagree. Noah's wife was, indeed, still home.

Brandon sighed heavily. "You're probably right. I'll talk to her."

"Things will work out," Noah said. "The important thing is that she's home."

Brandon's belly clenched. No, the important thing was that she stayed.

Muffled voices greeted Jana as she descended the curving staircase, piquing her curiosity. She'd just returned home from another day with her aunt, the clock was about to strike six and someone had come to visit? Calling hours ended at five. A tremor of unease swept through her. Had something happened at Aunt Maureen's after she left?

Or had Brandon actually come home on time?

At the foot of the stairs Jana saw Charles in the foyer talking with a tall, slender man, not much older than herself, respectably dressed in a decent, though not expensive, suit. The men quieted as Jana approached.

"Good evening, Mrs. Sayer," Charles intoned. "This gentleman has come to call on Mr. Sayer."

The man pulled off his bowler and pressed it

against his chest, holding the brim with both hands. Small, round eyeglasses reflected the glow of the wall sconces.

"Please forgive my intrusion, Mrs. Sayer," he said, changing the grip on his bowler. "My name is Fisk. Oliver Fisk."

"I explained to Mr. Fisk," Charles said, "that Mr. Sayer isn't home."

"How is it you know my husband?" Jana asked, walking closer.

"I'm a business associate. Well, actually, I'm an employee," he said. "I'm the editor of the *Los Angeles Messenger*. The newspaper."

With his slender frame and bookish appearance Jana thought he looked more like an accountant or librarian.

Fisk fidgeted with his hat. "Mr. Sayer owns the paper, as you know...or perhaps don't know, since I'm sure you're much too busy to concern yourself with matters of business. That's not to imply that you're flighty or ignorant, but rather—"

"Mr. Fisk," Jana said, taking pity on him. "Would you care to come in and wait for my husband?"

Rather than looking relieved, Oliver's anxiety ratcheted up another notch. He drew in a breath, seemingly searching for, and finding, a dose of courage.

"Yes," he proclaimed. "Yes, I'd like to do just that. I'd like to wait for him."

"Charles, would you be kind enough to have some refreshment sent to the sitting room?" Jana asked.

"Yes, ma'am," he replied and relieved Oliver of his bowler.

"Please come this way, Mr. Fisk."

She led him down the hallway to the sitting room she liked and seated herself on the settee. Oliver folded his long, ungainly arms and legs into the chair across from her with little grace.

"I can't promise when…my husband…will arrive," Jana said, the term odd on her tongue. It wasn't pleasant admitting, even to this stranger, that she had no idea what Brandon's schedule was.

"I don't mean to cause trouble," Oliver fretted, though he'd done nothing that required an apology. "I've tried numerous times to see Mr. Sayer at his office, but I've been unsuccessful. And I must speak with him right away. That's why I took this chance of coming here, to his home, even without an invitation, this late in the day."

Something about Oliver Fisk touched Jana's heart. "Is there a problem at the newspaper?"

"Yes, there's a problem. Very much so." He nodded his head vigorously. "Mr. Sayer is closing it."

Jana's eyes widened. "The newspaper? Brandon is closing the newspaper?"

"It hasn't been as prosperous as any of us would have liked," Oliver admitted. "But I can turn things around. I know I can. If Mr. Sayer would just give me a little more time I could make the *Messenger* the premier newspaper in the city."

Jana suddenly understood why she'd seen Brandon reading two newspapers at breakfast. Comparing the *Messenger* to the very popular *Times*, no doubt.

"I'll be the first to say that I lack a great deal of experience in the newspaper game," Oliver said, lacing and unlacing his long fingers. "But when the editor position fell to me, I was confident I could make a go of it. I still am. All I need is more time."

"That sounds reasonable to me," Jana agreed. "In fact, it seems to me that—"

Brandon strode into the room as if he were a force of nature, bringing both Jana and Oliver Fisk to their feet, commanding their attention with his very presence. He wasn't happy. Jana wasn't sure who Brandon was more annoyed to find in his sitting room: the newspaper editor—or her.

A tense silence froze the room as Brandon glared at them both, then settled his gaze on Jana.

"Would you excuse us?" he asked, though it was a command not a request.

"But Charles is bringing us refreshment—"

"No, he's not." Brandon's gaze drilled into her. "Would you *please* excuse us?"

The unreasonable fear that had tickled her stomach hardened into a knot of anger. Jana felt her shoulders square and her chin go up a notch. Yet she didn't want to make a scene in front of Oliver Fisk.

"Good evening, Mr. Fisk," she said, managing to sound pleasant as her temper simmered, and left the sitting room feeling as if she'd abandoned the gentle editor.

In the foyer she saw Charles lingering. He didn't make eye contact with her—he never did—but at least he had the good grace to look uncomfortable that he'd ignored her request for refreshments on Brandon's orders.

Jana pounded up the staircase, resisting the urge to work off her anger by taking the steps two at a time, and fetched the small book she'd brought with her from Aunt Maureen's hotel suite today. She took the back stairs down to the kitchen, her footsteps echoing on the bare, wooden risers.

The cook, Mrs. Boone, was busy at the stove while her two assistants chopped vegetables at one of the worktables. The kitchen, equipped to prepare everything from intimate family meals to elegant affairs for hundreds of guests, dwarfed the three women. The aroma of the soon-to-be-served supper mingled with the steam rising from the pots.

Mrs. Boone's eyes narrowed as Jana approached. Of all the servants still in the household, Jana was sorry to see that Mrs. Boone was among them. A gray-haired, sturdy woman, Mrs. Boone ruled her kitchen with an iron hand. She had no use for suggestions from anyone, including Jana.

But that was fourteen months ago, Jana reminded herself.

"Good evening, Mrs. Boone," she said.

The woman gave her a curt nod. "Evening, Mrs. Sayer."

"I wanted to speak with you about the menus," Jana began and held up the book. "I have some new recipes here that I'd like you to incorporate into the meal."

"As it should be obvious to almost anyone," Mrs. Boone said, and jerked her thumb toward the stove, "supper is fully underway, requiring my whole attention. I don't have time to be discussing things at the moment."

From the corner of her eye, Jana saw the two assistants glance at her, then turn away quickly.

"There's nothing to discuss," Jana told her, placing the book on the sideboard beside the stove. "These are the recipes. Include them in this week's meals."

Mrs. Boone shook her head. "Mr. Sayer likes his meals just so…in case you don't know. He doesn't cater to fancy food or newfangled dishes. Did he tell you to make these changes?"

Jana pressed her lips together. "No," she admitted.

Mrs. Boone picked up the recipe book, gave it a cursory glance and handed it back to Jana. "When Mr. Sayer says it's all right to change something, then I'll change it."

The cook turned back to the stove, ending their conversation.

Jana's cheeks warmed, and not from the heat of the cookstove. She turned sharply and left the kitchen.

Fourteen months had passed…and nothing had changed.

As Jana passed Brandon's study, she spotted him at his desk, flipping through papers. He had, apparently, already dispatched Oliver Fisk. And that didn't suit Jana.

She walked into the study, Brandon's earlier dismissal and the cook's blatant disregard for her instructions still stinging.

"Why are you shutting down the *Messenger*?" she asked.

Brandon looked up. "You needn't concern yourself with business matters."

She stood in front of his desk. "I want to know."

"It's complicated."

"I'm certain I can follow."

He studied her for a moment, then sat back in his chair. "I purchased the newspaper two years ago. It was a strong rival for the *Times*. A few months later, the editor died. The paper floundered. A succession of editors couldn't revive it. Oliver Fisk is the latest to try."

"But you won't give him the time he needs?" Jana asked, hearing the edge on her voice.

Brandon heard it too, obviously, because he sat forward again and began rummaging through the desk. "I gave him six months to show an improvement. That hasn't happened."

"Then give him more time."

"I did." Brandon opened a lower drawer. "I gave him two additional months—three times."

"But if even more time is needed—"

"No more time." Brandon closed the drawer with a thud and looked up at Jana. "The *Messenger* is losing money every minute of every day. I won't tolerate that sort of loss any longer. Fisk has another six weeks to turn the paper around, or it will be closed. Permanently."

"But what about all the employees?" Jana asked. "You can't put those people out of work."

"Most of them will find jobs at the *Times*. The others might find work at one of my other businesses," Brandon said.

"And you won't even consider giving Mr. Fisk another extension?"

"It won't matter," Brandon said. "If that newspaper could have been saved, it would have happened already. It's a lost cause. Besides, I already have another project in the works for the Jennings Building. It's coming along nicely. Once the newspaper is closed and moves out, I can go forward with it."

"But that's hardly a reason—"

"It's the only reason I need." Brandon came to his feet, the tone of his words and the look on his face ending their conversation. "And in the future, when someone such as Oliver Fisk shows up here, you are not to offer them any hospitality whatsoever."

Jana's simmering anger flared. "Are you telling me I cannot be civil to whomever comes to the house?"

"Yes, that's exactly what I'm telling you." Brandon softened his voice. "It's all right...this time. You didn't know."

Jana just looked at him, too stunned to speak.

Brandon came around the desk. "There's something

else I want to talk to you about. Last night you said I had no idea about why you left. I thought about that today."

"You did?" Now she was truly stunned.

"Yes. I thought about it and I want you to know that I'm fully aware of why you left."

A different sort of unease came over Jana. "You are?"

Brandon straightened his shoulders. "It was my fault, really. I didn't give you enough guidance. You were young and somewhat pampered, and I should have provided more direction, made you more aware of your duties and responsibilities."

She raised an eyebrow. "Oh, really?"

"Yes." He cleared his throat. "As I said, it was really my fault. It was my duty as your husband to provide those things. I was remiss in not doing so."

Her expression soured. "How generous of you to admit it."

"Yes. Well, I want to assure you the situation will be corrected. So," he said, drawing in a breath, "with your— and my—new commitment to our marital responsibilties, I'm sure everything will be fine. This time."

A thousand retorts jetted through Jana's mind, itching to be spoken, hurled at him like spiked daggers.

But she held her tongue. A sense of calm came over Jana.

"You have no idea how relieved I am to hear you say that," she said softly, never meaning anything more in her life.

Brandon smiled, apparently pleased with himself. "Good. I'm glad that settled things."

"Oh, that settled things, all right."

Jana left the study, determination and strength lengthening her strides as she bounded up the stairs and into her room.

Yes, Brandon's assessment settled things, all right. But not the way he thought.

Jana drew in a deep, cleansing breath, knowing without a doubt what would happen next.

She'd leave.

Nothing had changed in the past fourteen months—including Brandon. Everything that had driven her from the house was still firmly in place.

The servants who ignored her instructions.

That awful decorator Mr. McDowell who bullied her.

Not being allowed to have guests in her own home.

The loneliness.

The loneliness had been the hardest. She'd left all her friends behind in San Francisco when Brandon had brought her here. Aunt Maureen, hundreds of miles away. Everything that was familiar, friendly, comforting.

And Brandon, always gone. Up early, not wanting her presence at the breakfast table. Out late, business keeping him occupied well into the evenings.

Crying alone in her bed at night.

He had seemed almost a stranger during those first three months, always busy, in a rush, hurrying off to attend to something important. She hadn't felt she could approach him about anything—certainly not her unhappiness.

Jana drew herself up and took a deep breath. She wasn't crying anymore.

Perhaps nothing in this house had changed in the past fourteen months, but she certainly had. The decision she'd made in London now looked all the more correct.

She absolutely would not live her life under these circumstances.

She was leaving.

Jana pressed her lips together. She'd never last the remaining four weeks under this roof. Yet she'd given her word, committed to stay. Her only escape would be Brandon himself releasing her from her promise.

A slow smile spread across Jana's mouth. Brandon would ask her to leave.

She'd see to it.

Chapter Six

"Good morning." Jana breezed into the breakfast room, her smile as cheery as the sun streaming in through the lace-covered windows.

Brandon's gaze came up from the two newspapers on the table in front of him, frowning slightly.

"Jana, I thought we agreed that I was to have breakfast alone. You know I need this time to think over the day, get a jump—"

"I was simply too excited to wait." Jana yanked out the chair at his right elbow and planted herself in it. "First of all, I have to thank you for clarifying things for me last night. I realized you're absolutely right. We both must live up to our duties and responsibilities if our marriage is going to work."

Brandon nodded thoughtfully. "Good. I'm relieved to hear you say that."

"Yes, I thought you would be." Jana plucked a grape

from the fruit bowl on the table and popped it into her mouth. "And I'm glad we're in agreement."

Brandon's gaze lingered on her lips. "Well, huh, yes, so am I."

Jana took another grape, rolled it against her lips, then pushed it into her mouth, her finger lingering a few seconds between her lips.

"So, today," she went on, rubbing her lips together, "we will both go forth with a new commitment to our roles as husband and wife. I'm excited."

Brandon shifted in the chair. "I'm growing excited myself."

"I'm starting on the house today. The decorating is long overdue. I intend to give it my full attention. Nothing will be left undone." Jana selected a banana from the serving bowl, peeled it and slid it past her lips. She paused, not biting into it, and pulled it out again. "If that's all right with you, of course."

"Huh?"

She touched her tongue to the tip of the banana. "Do I have free rein to decorate the house?"

He just looked at her.

"Brandon? The decorating? *Brandon?*"

He dragged his gaze from her lips up to her eyes, then ran his finger under his shirt collar. "Oh, yes, the decorating. Of course. Do whatever you want. The house is yours."

"And you'll take care of the grounds?" Jana asked, biting slowly into the banana.

He gulped, his gaze dropping to her mouth again. "What…whatever you want."

Jana chewed slowly, then swallowed. "The grounds, like so many other things here, are in need of some long overdue attention. Wouldn't you agree?"

His breathing picked up. "Oh, hell yeah…"

"I'll inform the gardeners of the changes I want, and you'll oversee their work, if that's all right with you." She closed her lips around the banana once more and bit into it.

"Certainly…"

She swallowed quickly, laid the banana aside and jumped to her feet. "Excellent. I'll get started immediately."

"You're—you're leaving?" He came out of his chair.

"Duties and responsibilities call," she said briskly and snatched up both newspapers from the table. "I'll need these."

Brandon looked at the spot where the newspapers had lain, then up at her. "What for?"

"As I recall, the *Times* has the best advertisements for all those fabulous stores along Wilshire." Jana waved her hand about the room. "Brandon, I have an entire house to decorate."

"What about the *Messenger*?" he asked, gesturing lamely to the other newspaper.

"After you explained to me last night about the situation with the *Messenger*, I wanted to look it over, see if I can discern exactly what you mean," Jana explained.

"But I always read the newspaper on the way to the office," Brandon said.

"I'm sure that after our breakfast together this morning, you'll have plenty to occupy your mind." She flicked the tip of her tongue along her bottom lip, gave him a slow smile, and left the breakfast room.

"Jana! Wait!"

She turned back to see Brandon hurry after her. His cheeks were slightly flushed and a tiny drop of perspiration hung in his sideburn.

She'd seen those things before.

Brandon eased closer. "Does our new commitment to our duties and responsibilities include a resumption of our…marital relations?"

She frowned thoughtfully, then nodded. "Oh, you mean our lovemaking. As we used to do. You and me rolling around beneath the covers until the wee of the morning? All those delightfully sinful moments we shared?"

His breathing quickened. "Yes?"

"Hum…" Jana tapped her finger against her lips. "Perhaps we could consider that."

"Now?"

She tsked. "Brandon, we have our responsibilities to see to today."

"Yes, but—"

She touched his chest with the newspaper. "Let's discuss it at supper tonight, shall we?"

"I'll be home early," he promised.

Jana gave him a saucy little grin and left him standing in the doorway.

"What the hell!"

Brandon's roar rang through the house, down the hallway and into the sitting room, bringing Jana up out of her chair.

Though she felt a little guilty about her blatant flirting and not-so-subtle innuendo this morning at the breakfast table, she'd assuaged her conscience today with the conviction of her decision: if she couldn't get him to stay home, she could never torment him enough so that he'd ask her to leave.

She glanced at the mantel clock and smiled to herself. Just past the stroke of six and Brandon was home.

So far, her plan was working beautifully.

Jana left the sitting room and found Brandon in the foyer glaring at the scaffolds, reams of wallpaper, cans of paint, tools, equipment and the dozen workmen extending down the hallway.

"Good evening, Brandon," she greeted him, a placid smile on her face. It wasn't easy holding that expression in place against Brandon's scowl, even though she'd expected it in this next phase of her plan.

"What the hell is going on?" he demanded, raising his voice over the din of banging hammers and grinding saws.

"I'm decorating," she said. "Remember? We discussed it at breakfast this morning."

"This isn't *decorating*!"

"It's the way *I* decorate," she said crisply. "I'm knocking out a few of the walls."

"Knocking out the—*what*?" He gaze pinged around, then turned back at her. "Jana, you can't knock out a—"

She drew herself up a little. "You told me this morning that I could do whatever I wanted with the house."

He blinked. "I said that?"

"Oh, yes. My mind reeled with the possibilities. After all, you put me in charge of this project so I want to do my very best to please you. And, of course, to live up to my duty as your wife."

Brandon's gaze crawled over the workmen. "I never said you could do all of *this*."

"But you did put me in charge of the house, correct?"

"Yes, of course, I did. But—"

"And you do expect me to take my responsibilities seriously?"

"Yes—"

"And it is my duty as your wife to take over the house, is it not?"

"Well, yes, but—"

"Good. I'm glad I have your approval. Come along. I want you to see everything I'm doing."

Jana led the way down the hallway, skirting workmen, stepping over tools, and stopped at the doorway to the parlor. She waved her arm.

"I'm taking out those two walls, widening this whole wing of the house and lowering the floor."

"Lowering the—"

"And wait until you see what I'm doing to your study."

"My study?" Brandon bristled further. "My study is—"

"—part of the house, correct?"

"Well, yes, but—"

"I take the responsibilities you've given me very seriously, Brandon," she informed him. "I'm reworking the entire house, which includes your study. Come, I'll show you."

Jana ducked under ladders and sidestepped scaffolding until she reached Brandon's study. With the furniture pushed to the center of the wall and shrouded beneath a tarp, three carpenters stripped the walls, ceiling and floors.

Brandon pressed his palm against his forehead, his eyes wide. "What the...?"

"I'm renovating the entire room, floor to ceiling. For you," Jana announced.

"Where the hell am I supposed to work?"

"I found you a new spot," Jana told him. "A room off the kitchen."

He frowned. "What room?"

"The one next to the pantry."

"That's a storage room."

"It will be cozy. You'll feel snug in there," Jana assured him. "Your things are already in place...those that fit, anyway."

"This is unacceptable," Brandon declared. "I need a place to work."

She gazed up at him. "Didn't you say we both had to accept our responsibilities? Are you saying you're not willing to do that?"

"Of course, but—"

"Then you understand that we both have to make a few minor adjustments to get our marriage back on track. Isn't that what you want?"

"I need my study," he insisted.

"And you'll have it," she assured him. "I'm instructing the carpenters to make this room their first priority. Now, here's what I'm doing with your study. You'll love it. It's going to be pink."

"Pink?"

"Pink."

"Pink?"

"It's the rage in Europe. I don't know why it hasn't caught on here yet," Jana declared. She gestured to the walls. "There'll be a mural of lambs and ducks over there, and cherubs frolicking on clouds on the ceiling. It will be very soothing."

Brandon closed his eyes, pressed his fingertips against his temples and rubbed little circles. He drew in a breath and looked at Jana.

"When you said you were going to decorate, I didn't think you meant—"

"See? You've just proved my point. You're tense and anxious after a hard day at the office, and the new, more restful motif in your study will be just the thing to relax you."

He blew out a tired breath. "Jana, I don't—"

"The workmen are leaving momentarily."

"Good," he mumbled, releasing a heavy sigh.

"Our guests are arriving shortly."

He jerked upright again. "Guests? Tonight? You know I prefer quiet evenings at home."

"A man in your position has social obligations, all of which have been overlooked for far too long," Jana told him. "But don't worry, I'm taking charge of that also. Just as you wanted."

Jana strode off down the hallway toward the kitchen. "Do change your shirt," she called, not looking back.

When she reached the kitchen door she paused and glanced back. Brandon stood among the disarray, the pounding hammers and grinding saws, rubbing his forehead.

A pang of guilt swept through her. She'd never seen him look so distressed. For an instant she wanted to shout at the workmen to leave, take Brandon to the sitting room, place a cool cloth on his head.

But Jana did none of those things. She pushed into the kitchen hoping with all her heart that Brandon would ask her to leave soon. This plan of hers was harder to execute than she imagined.

Chapter Seven

He couldn't remember a more miserable evening.

Slumped in his office desk chair, Brandon threaded his fingers together across his chest, remembering the hellish evening he'd spent last night—in his own home, no less.

Bad enough that he'd walked in on the complete chaos of workmen, loud noises and flying sawdust. Then he'd had to endure supper with two young women he didn't know and whose names he'd forgotten before the soup was served.

Friends of Jana's, she'd explained shortly before their arrival. She'd run into them that morning while shopping on Wilshire and invited them for supper. Brandon had hardly been able to get through the meal for all their incessant chatter about fabric, hats and closet space.

He'd have left the table had it not been for Jana's gown—or, more accurately, Jana's bosom.

The familiar craving claimed him once more, just as it had all evening, all during the night and all morning. His desire for Jana simmered, bubbling up over and over by thoughts of her continually popping into his head. He'd cancelled an appointment today to hide out in his office, not thinking himself fit to be seen in public.

Oh, God, how he wanted her.

He'd done an admirable job of controlling himself, he thought, since her return. Not an easy undertaking, given that she was under his roof, steps away, even more beautiful and voluptuous than when she'd left fourteen months ago.

Yes, he'd managed just fine until last night…until she showed up at the supper table in that gown.

Brandon ached anew at the recollection of sitting at the opposite end of the table from her with a nearly unfettered view of his wife's breasts which threatened to escape her bodice at any moment.

Or so he'd caught himself hoping.

He'd never seen the amethyst gown on her before so he figured she'd purchased it while in Europe. Perhaps the style was different there, gowns cut lower than usual. Her creamy white skin had shone in the lamplight, glistening against the dark purple fabric of the gown. Her full, plump breasts undulated with each breath, each movement, mesmerizing him.

He'd nearly groaned aloud when she reached for the salt.

Jana had magnificent breasts. He remembered that

from their first three glorious months together. But somehow, they looked bigger now.

Or perhaps it was just that he hadn't seen them in a while. Or touched them. Or—

A brisk knock sounded on his office door and Noah Carmichael stepped into the room. Brandon rolled his chair farther under his desk, and grumbled, "What do you want?"

Noah frowned. "Still no marital bliss, huh?"

"I know you have an office in this building, so why don't you stay there?" Brandon asked, squaring off the stacks of papers and ledgers on his desk.

"I take it the answer to my question is no," Noah said, settling into a chair in front of Brandon's desk. He held out a piece of paper. "Several more people interested in the Jennings Building. You and I are going to make a fortune on this thing."

Brandon snatched the paper from his hand and, after a cursory glance, slapped it down. "I don't know why the hell it should be so difficult to have a wife."

"No honeymoon," Noah told him.

Brandon pressed his lips together to stifle a moan as another wave of wanting swelled in him.

"You should have taken Jana on a honeymoon," Noah continued. "Just the two of you. Endless days of mindless lovemaking. Nothing to do but burrow beneath the covers and—"

"At the time, I had a very important business deal in the works," Brandon blurted out. He drew in a breath, trying to control himself. "I asked Jana to pick a different wedding day, but she insisted that particular date was important to her."

"Too bad," Noah said, then sighed wistfully. "Honeymoons are important—tiring, but important."

"Yes, well, thank you so much for your brilliant insight," Brandon grumbled, "but it's a little late for that. Right now, I have to deal with the problem at hand."

"Which is?"

"She's redecorating the house. And she's inviting guests for supper."

"Damn her…"

Brandon threw him a sour look. "Everything in my life is in disarray."

"That's half the fun of having a wife," Noah said.

Brandon shook his head. "Perhaps she needs more guidance."

"Perhaps she needs a distraction."

"Such as?" Brandon asked.

"Get her pregnant."

Brandon groaned aloud and felt another wave of heat engulf him.

"Believe me, I know from where I speak," Noah said, giving him a proud smile. "Beth's expecting."

"You're—you're going to be a father?" Brandon offered his hand across the desk, hoping Noah wouldn't notice that he didn't rise from his chair. "Congratulations."

"Thank you," Noah said, looking altogether pleased with himself. "Beth is consumed with the upcoming arrival. And, I admit, I'm rather excited about it too. So, keep that in mind when you get home this evening."

"Thanks…" Brandon sank back in his chair as Noah left the office, closing the door behind him. He sat in the silence, only the noise from the street reaching his ears. The need to go to the window, to stare out, pulled at him, bringing with it recollections from long ago, memories that never left him alone.

So many windows in so many houses. Standing on furniture, peering out. Watching. Waiting. Hoping…

Brandon pushed himself out of the chair with such force that it banged into the wall behind him. If anyone needed a distraction right now, it was him. He shoved a few items into his satchel and left the office, barking to Mr. Perkins as he rushed past.

In the hallway he ignored the birdcage elevator and took the stairs to the ground floor. He hit the street and walked north, forcing himself to take in the surroundings. Perhaps something would strike his fancy—another business opportunity he hadn't yet noticed in the city.

But other thoughts invaded his mind.

Fine thing, Noah had already gotten his wife pregnant and Brandon couldn't even get his wife into bed. Maybe he could change that. It would certainly go a long way toward improving his life.

Yesterday morning after breakfast Jana had said they could discuss resuming their marital relations. There'd been no time for such a talk last night, with the house full of those silly women until all hours.

Brandon drew in a breath. It was high time they got on with the discussion.

"Mrs. Sayer!"

Jana paused amid the swirl of pedestrians on Broadway, turning toward the sound of her name. Dozens of faces passed around her, men in suits and work clothes, women in fashionable attire or trailing children in their wake. Her gaze bounced from one to another, then settled on the familiar face of Oliver Fisk, the *Messenger*'s soon-to-be unemployed newspaper editor.

"Mrs. Sayer, how good of you to stop," Oliver said, touching the brim of his bowler.

They stepped into the shade cast by an office building as the sun dropped lower in the sky. Oliver wore the same jacket she'd seen him in before, but it looked freshly pressed, neat and clean, like Oliver himself.

"I'm pleased to see you again, Mr. Fisk," she said.

"On the way to your husband's office?"

An odd feeling crept over Jana. Brandon's office was nearby?

"The Bradbury Building," Oliver said, nodding up the street. "There, on the corner."

She threw a glance in that direction. "Oh, yes, of course."

"Possibly the finest office building in the city," Oliver said. Then his cheeks flushed. "But you already know that."

Actually, she didn't. Jana stole another look up the

block. If Brandon had ever told her his office was located there, she'd forgotten it.

"May I have the honor of walking you there?" Oliver asked.

He thought it odd, Jana was sure, to find her on the street alone. Though Los Angeles was civilized enough, decent women most always had an escort of some sort.

"Thank you, Mr. Fisk, but I'm headed elsewhere," she replied with a gracious smile. A smile that she hoped kept hidden the fact that she'd just come from the Morgan Hotel around the corner and another visit with her aunt. No one, not even Brandon, knew her aunt was in town. Brandon, apparently, assumed her aunt had gone to her own home in San Francisco while Jana had traveled to Los Angeles. It suited Jana's purposes that her aunt was a homebody, content in the hotel's suite, and no one—especially Brandon—knew she was in town.

"I was doing some shopping," Jana explained, thinking she'd be better off changing the subject. "I'm headed home now."

Oliver cast a quick glance around but saw no waiting coach or carriage, since none existed. If he thought it strange—and why wouldn't he?—he said nothing.

"I've been reading the *Messenger*," Jana said.

He gave her a brave smile. "Always glad to meet a reader, one of the dwindling few."

"I understand you have another six weeks to turn things around," Jana said.

His smile grew more brave. "I'm giving it everything I've got…although, I fear it's a lost cause."

"But with six weeks you can—"

"Mr. Sayer already has plans for the building."

Jana remembered Brandon telling her that. "They're tentative though, aren't they?"

"In theory, yes. But in reality…" Oliver drew in a breath. "Your husband is already going forward with the Jennings project. He's commissioned an architect to renovate the building, and is lining up new tenants."

"But that hardly seems fair," Jana said.

"I'm not giving up," Oliver said, squaring his slim shoulders. "If I can make a significant increase in circulation and boost advertising, Mr. Sayer will have to keep the *Messenger*'s presses running."

All that hardly seemed likely in six weeks. And even if Oliver achieved it, would Brandon abandon his Jennings project after he'd paid what surely was a large retainer to the architect? Backing out of the project would be expensive, to say nothing of the blow to Brandon's reputation. Jana feared the newspaper, and Oliver Fisk's career, were doomed.

But she put on a hopeful face for him. "I'm sending good thoughts your way, Mr. Fisk."

"Thank you, Mrs. Sayer," he replied, then drew himself up a bit. "My uncle was the original editor of the *Messenger*. A brilliant newspaperman. I only wish I'd had time to learn more from him before his death. But I'm soldiering on. That newspaper is his legacy. I can't let it go without a fight. I'm praying for a miracle."

"Good for you," Jana said, hoping she sounded encouraging when, in fact, she couldn't share his optimism.

Oliver Fisk would need a miracle to save his beloved newspaper.

Just as Brandon had done, Jana had read the *Messenger* and the *Times* side by side. And the truth was, the *Messenger* was just plain boring. It covered the same stories as the *Times*—political and business news, world events, local happenings. But the coverage wasn't as thorough, the stories not as well written. Nothing about the newspaper, to Jana's mind, would beckon new readers or sustain loyal ones.

"Good day, Mrs. Sayer." Oliver tipped his hat once more and left her standing on the sidewalk. She waited until he disappeared into the crowd, then went to the corner and waited for the trolley back to West Adams Boulevard.

When she arrived home, Charles met her in the vestibule and mumbled a greeting.

"Good evening, Charles, I—"

"You're *late*."

Jana turned at the sound of Brandon's voice. He stood at the edge of the foyer, his shoulders rigid, his jaw tight.

"You're late," he said again. "You're supposed to be home by six o'clock, and you're late."

Jana glanced at the clock that sat on the marble side table. Four minutes past the hour.

"You said you'd be home before six," Brandon said. "You said you would. You promised. I've—I've been waiting."

Her first thought was to point out the very few minutes and scoff at his concern—not to mention his silly request. But something in his tone, in his expression stopped her.

She read no anger in it. Nor was there concern for her safety, worry that something had befallen her, causing her lateness. Was it betrayal? Vulnerability?

A little of both, she realized.

Where fourteen months ago Jana might have gone crying to her room over his disapproval, now her heart softened and the desire to comfort him rose in her.

Jana went to him and gazed up at his tense expression. "It wasn't my intention to upset you," she said in her most soothing tone. She touched her palm to his cheek. "Let's go into the sitting room and I'll send for some tea."

For an instant, Brandon leaned into her palm, then pulled away as if embarrassed that he'd made a fuss, or that he'd allowed her to see his hidden need.

It startled Jana and caused a new sort of ache to tighten around her heart. Brandon had always been this way, emotionally withdrawn, and she'd just now realized it. Courted by him, married to him, bound to him as only a man and woman can be, and she'd never noticed it before.

How little she knew of the man who was her husband.

"Let's go have tea," Jana said gently. "We have time."

Brandon's expression clouded. "You didn't invite people for supper again, did you?"

For an instant, Jana was sorry that she had. Sorry that she'd upset him, sorry that his quiet evening would be interrupted.

But then she remembered all the lonely evenings she'd endured fourteen months ago—and all that awaited her if she stayed in this marriage.

"Yes, the Gentrys are coming," Jana said.

Brandon cursed. "I hate those people. Bob Gentry is overbearing. That wife of his is self-absorbed, and they're both opportunistic, ingratiating—"

"They'll arrive at seven. I have to go change." Jana started the staircase, then looked back. "I sent the landscape foreman to your office today to discuss the plans for the gardens, but he said you refused to see him."

"I didn't know he was there." Brandon shrugged. "Mr. Perkins must have refused to let him in."

"Brandon, we agreed that you'd oversee the landscaping," Jana said. "It is your responsibility, you know."

"Of course I know, but—"

"I hope in the future you'll show a little more commitment to your duties."

Jana hurried up the staircase, not waiting for a reply, but feeling Brandon's hot gaze following her.

Supper was tiring and irritating. Halfway through the meal, Jana disliked the Gentrys as much as Brandon did.

This morning when she was trying to come up with someone to invite to supper, a couple who would annoy Brandon to no end, the Gentrys seemed the obvious choice. She remembered them from the first three months of marriage when she'd been trying to fit into Brandon's social circle. The Gentrys were, indeed, opportunistic, the only couple Jana knew who would accept a supper invitation on a few hours' notice.

Now that they'd departed, she was glad to see them gone. She headed up to her room wondering if, for her own peace of mind, she should think of a different way to annoy her husband.

"Jana?"

She stopped outside the door to her bedchamber, surprised to see Brandon striding up the staircase and through the hallway toward her. Since her first night back in the house when she'd told him not to expect any intimacy between them, he'd made himself scarce when she'd retired for the evening.

She braced herself, expecting an earful over her choice of supper guests, but Brandon looked unruffled, as he approached, calm, thoughtful…

Handsome.

For an instant Jana gave in to the feeling, let it wind through her, coil around her heart.

Good-looking, smart, successful, ambitious. What woman wouldn't be attracted to such a man? As a girl of nineteen, Jana had been entranced by those qualities. But for a woman of twenty-one, they weren't nearly enough.

Brandon stopped in front of her, not coming too close, and slid his hands into his trouser pockets.

"The Gentrys were…"

"Obnoxious?" she suggested.

Brandon grinned, sending a shiver arrowing through Jana's heart. He smiled so seldom.

"At least now people will know I actually have a wife," he said, lifting his wide shoulders. "There was some talk…before…that I'd made you up. That I'd concocted an imaginary wife."

"No need to worry this time," Jana said. "I intend to keep up on social obligations—even if it means filling the house with couples like the Gentrys."

Brandon didn't protest, as she'd hoped. In fact, he said nothing at all, as if he hadn't heard her. Then she knew why.

He eased closer and his eyes darkened. A look Jana knew well.

"You look quite lovely tonight," Brandon said, his voice low and mellow.

Jana's heart picked up a little as he drew even nearer. She knew she should dart into her bedroom, yet something held her in place.

"I haven't seen you in this gown before," he said.

He glanced down at the low plunge of her garnet dress, his gaze alone making her breasts tingle, urging her to snuggle against his hard chest. She fought the temptation.

And thought herself doing an admirable job of resisting that temptation until Brandon drew even closer and the heat of his body covered her. He touched his palm to her cheek and leaned down. For a moment, his face remained only inches from her, his breath fanning her lips. Then he kissed her.

His mouth covered hers, warm and familiar, delicious and exciting. Jana opened her lips to him and he slipped inside, where he belonged. She sighed and rose on her toes. Brandon eased closer until their bodies met, then groaned deep in his throat. She looped his neck. He splayed his hand on her back and pulled her against him.

A hunger claimed Jana, alluring and demanding. She hadn't experienced it since—

Fourteen months ago.

Jana pulled away. Brandon's lips stayed with hers, then finally released them. They hung in their embrace for a few seconds, hot breath puffing against each other.

Jana stepped back. Heat throbbed in her cheeks. Her body warmed in old, familiar places that Brandon had brought to life fourteen months ago, and again now.

"I—I told you I didn't want us to resume our—our lovemaking," she said, her voice a breathy whisper. She kept her gaze down, unable to meet his eye.

"This is kissing," he said, a gentle teasing in his voice. "Lovemaking is something entirely different."

Jana looked up at him then. He lowered his head but didn't kiss her. Instead, he touched his cheek to hers, nuzzling her, brushing his lips against her.

His mouth played along the curve of her jaw, then dropped lower until his lips fanned her neck.

"If you've forgotten the difference between the two," Brandon murmured against her ear, "I'll be happy to demonstrate."

His lips claimed her neck once more, sending a rush through her. Jana closed her eyes for a moment, then drew in a breath and pushed away.

"No," she said, wanting to sound forceful but failing miserably.

Brandon didn't protest, but she saw the wanting in his darkened eyes, his heavy breath, his flushed cheeks. For an instant, Jana wanted to throw herself into his arms once more, have him carry her into her bedroom as he used to do.

But that would only complicate things. As Jana already knew, all too well.

Brandon seemed to read her thoughts. He backed up a step.

"I always thought we made a good-looking couple," Brandon said, his voice still low, heavy with need. "Both of us tall. A good match…physically. Did you like that about us, Jana? Before? Is that one of the things you liked about us? Surely, there was something…"

He'd asked her that question the first day she'd come to the house, when she wanted a divorce and he wanted to try again. Wasn't there something she liked about them as a couple?

"No, Brandon," she said, forcing strength in her

voice. She straightened away and pushed up her chin. "No. There was nothing I liked about us."

She turned and hurried into her room, closing the door behind her, not wanting to see his face.

Chapter Eight

Brandon sprang in Jana's mind the instant she opened her eyes the next morning. It didn't surprise her, given that he'd prowled her dreams all night.

She pushed herself higher on her pillows and yanked the coverlet up to her chin. Dozens of mornings—three months' worth—floated through her mind. Mornings when she'd awakened with Brandon in her bed. Mornings when they'd awakened together after a night of lovemaking.

Jana's stomach quivered at the memory. From the very first night they'd spent as husband and wife, Brandon had been gentle and coaxing and loving. Never in a hurry, never annoyed with her inexperience, never distracted from the moments they shared. Alone in her bedroom—they never made love in his room—Brandon forbade the servants to interrupt; there would never be a circumstance that warranted it, she'd overheard him say. Her room was their world.

From the whispers of her girlhood friends, Jana had learned the ways of men, how they visited their wives on occasion, then went on their way. Brandon never left her side. All night they lay together, listening to the rain or the wind, or watching the moon through the window as it arced through the heavens. In the morning, they awoke snuggled like kittens, and each morning Brandon whispered that he never, ever wanted to leave her. She believed him. She knew how he felt. She never wanted him to go.

But he always did. He walked out of her room and, in crossing the threshold, became a different person.

Jana gazed through the open curtains, out the window she and Brandon used to lie beneath. Her heart warmed at the memory of how handsome he was, how she treasured those moments, the feel of him next to her and the closeness she enjoyed.

But she couldn't remember one single thing they'd talked about.

Jana sat up. How could that be? She recalled in great detail nearly every word the overbearing decorator Mr. McDowell had said, each and every slur bestowed upon her by the cantankerous cook. She remembered the other women in her newly evolving social circle, those who'd been accepting, those who hadn't.

But she couldn't remember a conversation with her own husband?

Oliver Fisk flashed into her mind, and it vexed Jana to recall that the quite proper newspaper editor had known the location of Brandon's office, but she didn't.

Had she simply forced it all from her mind these last fourteen months?

Another sort of longing suddenly filled Jana's heart. Brandon had hardly been the biggest thing on her mind once she'd arrived in London.

A brief knock sounded on her door before it swung open and Abbie came inside.

"Morning, Mrs. Sayer," she said in greeting.

"Good morning, Abbie," Jana said, rising from the bed.

"How was your night?" Abbie glanced at the barely disturbed coverlet. "Uneventful, as usual, I see."

Jana smiled, finding Abbie's frankness refreshing. "And they will remain uneventful."

"It's not hardly my place to say, but if certain things go unattended for too long, well, they might go wandering off."

"Yes, I know...." Jana slipped her arms into the sleeves of her robe, troubled by the thought that Brandon would take his affections elsewhere, as any man would do, if she spurned him long enough. Even though she didn't intend to stay. Even though he'd certainly sought comfort from someone while she was gone.

"I suppose Brandon had...company...here while I was away," Jana said.

"Oh, no, ma'am."

She swung around to face Abbie as the maid opened the closet doors. "But surely—I mean he must have—"

"Mr. Sayer never brought a woman into this house," Abbie told her with such conviction that Jana believed her.

"I suppose he went elsewhere," Jana said.

"I suppose he would, being a man, and all," Abbie said. She shook her head. "But I've got my doubts. The way he pined after you..."

"What do you mean?"

Abbie hesitated a moment, then said, "After you left, I came in to clean, keep things looking nice, you know, just in case. And several times I found Mr. Sayer here, in your room...all alone."

Jana frowned. "Doing what?"

Abbie shrugged. "Just lying on the bed, sometimes. Or touching your things left on the bureau. I saw him standing at the window once, looking out, holding your pillow."

Jana reeled back, the vision filling her head, making it spin. Sorrow and guilt clutched her heart. She'd had no idea....

"Good morning."

Jana whirled toward the sound of Brandon's voice. He stood in the hallway, his head tilted to see around the partially opened door.

"Good—good morning," she said.

He stepped through the doorway as if he weren't sure he should, and his gaze bounced around the room.

Was he remembering their nights spent together

here? Jana wondered. Or the hours he'd wandered alone through her room in the wake of her departure.

"I thought you'd want to see this," Brandon said and held out a newspaper.

Jana glanced at the mantel clock and saw that it was past time for Brandon to have left for the office. Her dreams had caused her to oversleep.

"The advertisement," Brandon said, holding the newspaper out farther. "I thought you might want to see it."

Jana crossed the room and took the paper. Her fingers brushed his, making her keenly aware that she wore only her nightgown and robe—a fact not lost on Brandon, given the way his gaze traveled over her.

When she didn't answer, he stepped back. "I'm going to bed—" Brandon stopped, looked pained and said, "Downstairs. I'm going *downstairs* now."

She couldn't help but grin. He gave her one last lingering look, then strode away.

Jana leaned out the door, watching as he disappeared down the stairs, a part of her wishing that he'd stop, come back.

Then she admonished herself for having the thought and reminded herself to be on guard against him. So far, Brandon had respected her wishes about not sharing a bed. He'd held back.

She had to do the same…somehow.

"Dammit…"

Brandon cursed as he cradled the elbow he'd just

banged into the wall behind him. The storage room Jana had converted into his study barely held the makeshift desk, the spindly chair and a side table laden with a teetering stack of papers and ledgers. He'd hit his knee and banged his elbow twice as he tried to get some work done in the small, airless room.

He should have gone downtown to his office where he could be comfortable and actually get something accomplished. But after seeing Jana in her nightgown and robe this morning, he couldn't bring himself to leave the house. So here he was, crammed into this tiny room, waiting what he judged to be sufficient time for his wife to dress and come downstairs so he could see her again.

"Fine thing…" Brandon grumbled as he shifted in the tight space. Business—important business—awaited him, yet when Jana hadn't appeared at the breakfast table he had decided to delay leaving for the office. Then he'd come up with a silly notion of bringing her the newspaper just as an excuse to go to her room and see her—his own wife.

Of course, that hadn't turned out badly at all.

A warmth curled through Brandon at the memory of seeing Jana in her nightclothes. Nothing on underneath. The light streaming in the window behind her had provided him with an enticing glimpse of the curve of her hip through the thin fabric.

The craving that had plagued him for so long worsened. He remembered those hips. The way they curved gently, fitting the palm of his hand. Her long silken legs, sliding up and down his thighs. And her breasts.

Without a doubt Jana had the most beautiful breasts he'd ever seen—or imagined. If he'd caught sight of them in her room just now, he'd have—

"Hellfire."

Brandon shoved back his chair and surged to his feet, cracking his elbow against the wall once more. His head banged against the low-hanging light fixture.

"Dammit…" He stomped from the room, rubbing the spot on his head. "Jana! Jana!"

Charles scurried down the hallway toward him looking as concerned as the butler ever looked.

"Where's Jana?" Brandon demanded. "Is she still upstairs?"

"The kitchen, sir. I saw her go in the kitchen a moment ago," Charles said, and quickly stepped aside.

The kitchen? She'd dressed and come downstairs already? For some reason, that didn't suit Brandon either. He straight-armed the kitchen door and planted himself beside one of the worktables, prepared for the flurry of activity his unusual presence in the room always brought to the kitchen staff.

But no one noticed him. The attention of everyone—the cook's assistants, the grocer delivering at the back door and two maids—was riveted to Jana and Mrs. Boone who appeared to be in a standoff of sorts across the room. Neither woman looked happy.

"If you'll pardon me for saying so *again,* Mrs. Sayer," Mrs. Boone said, "I've been Mr. Sayer's cook for a very long time now."

"I'm well aware of that," Jana told her.

"I was here, you know, cooking for him the whole time you were gone. To wherever it was you ran off to," Mrs. Boone said. "And I can tell you that Mr. Sayer won't like any of those new recipes you want me to prepare."

Brandon bristled at the cook's tone. Mrs. Boone had been a loyal servant for a long time. He'd never heard her speak so disrespectfully to anyone before.

Then it occurred to him the reason for the confrontation. Jana was attempting to change the menus.

"You needn't concern yourself with my travel schedule. You should concern yourself with doing as you're instructed," Jana informed the cook. She dropped the small book on the sideboard with a thud. "These are the recipes I want you to use, and here is the menu I've written for this week. I expect meals to be prepared accordingly, beginning this evening."

With a crisp nod, Jana sailed past the cook and their audience of servants. Her footsteps faltered when she caught sight of Brandon, yet she didn't stop.

He followed her into the hallway.

"What the hell was that all about?" he asked, striding after her. "You're changing the menus?"

"Yes, I am."

"But I like the meals the way they are," Brandon insisted.

Jana stopped abruptly and swung around to face him. "The meals are my responsibility now, aren't they?"

"Yes. But you know I'm particular about the food—"

"The recipes needed updating. And what are you doing here?" she asked.

"I'm going to the office later," Brandon said, feeling a little odd that he was required to give an explanation.

"Fine. While you're here you can speak with the gardeners," Jana said and started walking again.

"Jana?" Brandon hurried after her. "Jana, wait. I want to talk to you."

She stopped, and he couldn't help but notice the most appealing flush to her cheeks. His body warmed anew at the recollection of Jana in her thin nightgown earlier this morning.

"What is it?" she asked.

"I, uh…" Brandon gaped at her, trying to remember.

"You wanted to talk with me?"

Brandon rubbed his forehead. "Yes. Yes, I did." He cleared his throat and straightened his shoulders. "How much longer before my study will be finished? That little room by the kitchen is intolerable."

"Let's go have a look," Jana said, and took off down the hallway again, leaving Brandon to trail after her.

The sound of hammers and saws greeted them as they drew closer to the study, this wing of the house in even more disarray than before, it seemed to Brandon.

He stopped at the entrance to the parlor. Inside, a dozen workmen balanced on scaffolds and ladders went about their jobs. But to Brandon, something was amiss.

"Weren't these men farther along on this job *yesterday?*" he asked.

At his elbow, Jana nodded. "Yes. But I changed my mind. I decided I didn't want the walls removed. I told the workers to put them up again."

"Put them up again?"

"And I don't want the floor lowered either," Jana said. "I decided to raise the ceiling instead."

"Raise the ceiling?" Brandon's eyes widened. "But there's another story over it. You can't just—"

"I've changed my mind about your study, too."

A thread of hope flickered in Brandon's chest. "Does that mean you're not making it pink?"

"I don't know what I was thinking," Jana mused, waving her hand to dismiss the entire idea.

"Thank God," Brandon mumbled.

"I've decided now to make it yellow."

"Yellow?"

"Yes. Pale yellow. A shade somewhere between sunflower and goldenrod," she said, touching her chin thoughtfully. "With a mural depicting bunnies with fluffy tails amid a field of pansies."

Brandon's shoulders sagged. "Let me guess. The workmen had to start—"

"—over. Yes." Jana gazed up at him. "I don't want to ask them to rush. I want your study to be just perfect for you, Brandon. No matter how long it takes."

"But, Jana—"

"Do talk with the gardeners before you leave," Jana said. "I'll see you tonight at supper."

"We're not having guests again, are we?"

"Of course," Jana announced. "You needn't worry, Brandon, I'm committed to establishing our rightful presence in the city's social scene."

He watched as she walked away, her bustle bobbing down the hallway. "Where are you going?" he called.

She paused and glanced back. "I have a full day of luncheons, teas and social calls."

"But—"

"Do be on time tonight," she said, then turned and walked away.

A little groan slipped through Brandon's lips as the sight of Jana's bobbing bustle disappeared around the corner. Unwanted supper guests. New meals. The house under construction. And a yellow study—with bunnies. The massive disruption of his schedule, his solitude, his accustomed surroundings. Jana was making his life miserable.

And still, he wanted her.

Chapter Nine

Another woman. Just what he needed today.

Brandon entered his office and spotted Leona Albright, resplendent in ivory and gold, languishing on the settee across the room.

At least this woman didn't torment him, unlike the one he'd left at home this morning.

"Brandon, dear, is this some sort of ruse you're attempting?" Leona asked. "Coming in late? Trying to make people think all sorts of delicious things about your morning activities at home?"

He pushed the door closed and dropped his satchel on his desk. "How is it that the most intimate details of my life have become public knowledge?"

"One only has to look at the scowl on your face, dear, to see what is—or isn't—going on."

Brandon turned to her. "Is that why you're here? To spread more rumors?"

The playful grin disappeared from Leona's face. "Brandon, you know that I—of all people—would never do that."

A pang of guilt twisted his gut. Yes, he knew that. And he was ashamed of himself for suggesting it.

"I'm sorry," he said quickly. "You've kept…things… to yourself for over twenty—"

"No reason to count years," Leona said quickly.

Brandon grinned at her vanity. Like many women, Leona considered the subject of age taboo. But it had, in fact, been over twenty years since Brandon had come to know Leona. He, a child. She, a new bride. It seemed so long ago now. And Europe so far away.

"Come. Sit." She patted the arm of the chair beside the settee. "We'll talk."

Brandon hesitated. Did he need to hear from another woman? Perhaps this one might actually help to make things better. He sat down.

"All right, then," Leona said, shifting on the settee as if settling in for a long stay. "As I recall, your wife returned only to announce that she wanted a divorce. You convinced her to stay, give the marriage another try."

Brandon nodded. "That's correct."

"So what's wrong? Isn't she genuinely trying?"

"No, actually, Jana is trying very hard," Brandon said. "She's taken over her duties and responsibilities at the house, just as I'd instructed."

One of Leona's eyebrows crept upward. "You *instructed* her?"

"Of course. That's why she left. I was remiss in my duty as her husband in providing direction."

"Oh, Brandon, dear…" Leona exhaled heavily and rolled her eyes. "So what is she doing now?"

"Everything I asked. Decorating the house, taking over with the servants, handling our social calendar."

"And you're happy with this?"

Brandon's expression soured. "I'm miserable. She's turned the whole house, my whole life, upside down."

A quiet moment passed before Leona spoke again. "It sounds as if your wife is planning to leave again."

An old familiar pain cut through Brandon causing a little groan to slip through his lips. Then he shook his head.

"No. No, Jana wouldn't do that," he insisted. "She has no reason to leave again."

"Have you given her a reason to *stay?*"

Brandon rubbed his forehead. "I don't know what you mean."

"Have you told her that you're glad she's home?"

"Well, no…"

"That you love her?"

"She knows I love her," Brandon said. "I married her, didn't I?"

"Have you told her you missed her?"

Brandon turned away, the question causing his belly to ache more.

Leona softened her voice. "Did you tell her that you stood by the window and watched for her? That you—"

"No." Brandon pushed himself out of the chair and

strode to the other side of the room, his back to
Leona. She didn't say anything else. She knew she'd
hit her mark.

"Your wife can go anywhere and perform the duties
and responsibilities that are expected of her," Leona
said. "Have you given her a reason to stay with you?"

"Damn…" Brandon turned away, pressing his lips together, struggling to hold in his stormy emotions.

"You really want her to stay, don't you?" Leona asked.

"Of course I do," Brandon said, a little too harshly.

"Why?"

"Because." He drew in a breath, struggling for words.
"Because I want a—a—"

"A normal life?"

"Yes."

"A home?"

Brandon turned to face Leona once more. "Yes. A
home," he said, getting the words out with some effort.
"That's why I married her. Jana was the most loving
creature I'd ever seen in my entire life. Full of caring
and goodness, optimism and happiness. She made me
believe love was possible. She embodied everything I'd
ever hoped for, ever dreamed of."

"So why aren't you trying harder to make things
work?" Leona asked.

"I am," Brandon insisted. "I told you, I've given her
direction. Explained her duties—"

"Have you forgotten that the sweet, innocent young
wife you remember has crossed the Atlantic and the

continent twice? She's lived abroad, made her own decisions, fended for herself and done so quite capably?"

"Her aunt was there also, helping her."

"At first, perhaps. But do you think your wife didn't
learn to handle things alone?" Leona proposed. "Has
she seemed meek and mild-mannered since her return?
Lost and unsure of herself?"

"No," Brandon said. "Not at all. In fact, she's rather
surprised me by the way she's grabbed hold of things
at home, taken charge."

"Then she doesn't need your guidance," Leona
concluded.

"Oh, God… Then she doesn't really need me for
anything, does she?" Brandon crossed the room and
collapsed into the chair once more.

"No," Leona said softly. "She doesn't *need* you for
anything. But, I suspect, she *wants* you—or did at one
time. I suspect, also, that she would like you to *need* her."

Brandon rubbed his forehead, fighting off another
tide of rising emotion. "No…"

Leona touched his arm. "You take risks in business
every day. You're going to have to risk your feelings—"

"No." He pulled his arm away and shook his head.

A moment passed before Leona spoke again. "If you
open your heart to Jana, expose your feelings and she
still turns you down, wouldn't you want to know that
about her?"

Brandon didn't answer.

"Wouldn't you want to take the risk that it might rekindle her feelings for you? That it might save your marriage?" Leona asked.

"I wouldn't know where to start," Brandon whispered.

"Start by telling her how you feel."

Brandon's gaze came up quickly. "Do you think it will make a difference?"

"I think you have to give it a try."

Leona rose from the settee. Brandon gazed up at her as she spoke again. "If, that is, you truly want your wife to stay."

Leona left the office.

Brandon remained in the chair, a witches' brew of emotion churning in him. Usually, he valued Leona's opinions. She was wise and informed. Little got past her. She'd proved herself a trusted confidante many times.

Dare he hope that this time, in these particular circumstances, she was wrong?

More than anything he wanted to settle back into his comfortable life with Jana. Fourteen months ago, marriage had been easy. Having a wife had been the simplest—and most wonderful thing—in his life. But everything had changed now.

Could Leona be right? Could Jana really be planning to leave him once more?

A quick rap sounded on his office door and Noah Carmichael strode inside.

"Invitation," he called as he dropped an envelope on Brandon's desk. "Beth said it's high time you brought your wife over for supper."

He turned to leave, but stopped in the doorway and looked back. "Are you all right?"

He considered confiding in Noah, asking for his advice. After all, Noah's marriage must be working out, since they had a baby on the way.

But Brandon couldn't bring himself to do it.

"Fine," Brandon replied, trying to put some enthusiasm into his voice so his friend wouldn't question him further. "I'm fine. Everything's fine."

"Don't forget to give Jana this invitation. I'll never hear the end of it if you don't," Noah said, then left the office.

Brandon rose from the chair and drew in a heavy breath. He had to admit that there was merit to the things Leona had just told him. And he knew what he had to do, if he wanted Jana to stay.

But could he bring himself to do it?

As plans went, this one was a good one. And it was proceeding perfectly.

Yet Jana wasn't happy.

Seated at the small writing desk in the sitting room, Jana sorted the stack of invitations into three piles, dealing them with a flick of her wrist as if they were playing cards. Everyone in the city, it seemed, had learned of her return and was anxious to draw her and Brandon into their social circle once more.

Jana eyed the three stacks before her. One held invitations from people she remembered from the early days of her marriage, people whose company she was certain she and Brandon would enjoy. The next contained invitations from people she doubted Brandon liked. The last, ones she knew he detested.

Glumly, Jana selected the last stack and began writing acceptance letters.

Yes, this plan she'd come up with to cause Brandon to ask her to leave was a good one. But it was starting to wear on her. It went against everything in her heart and in her mind to spend her time, energy and efforts to make someone's life miserable...even Brandon's life.

Jana wasn't sure how much longer she could keep it up. It didn't help that he was being reasonably nice about the whole thing. In fact, it made her feel worse.

Jana's heart ached a little recalling how distraught Brandon had been these past days over the workmen in the house, the horrendous supper guests she'd invited. She cringed at thinking about the outrageous meals she'd instructed Mrs. Boone to begin cooking this morning.

It took all her strength not to comfort him, at times. She wanted to touch him, caress him. She wanted to make things better for him.

But where would that get her?

Here. In the empty house. With an absent husband. Alone and miserable once more, just as she'd been the first three months of her marriage.

Jana straightened up and attacked the stack of correspondence with renewed fervor, and said a quick prayer that Brandon would see the futility of trying to continue their marriage and simply let her leave.

A noise from the hallway caught her ear and she looked up to see Brandon walking into the sitting room. Her gaze darted to the mantel clock. He wasn't due home for hours.

He looked tired, she thought, and wondered if his day had been a difficult one. For a moment, she wanted to go to him, have him sit on the settee beside her, soothe and comfort him.

But Jana held back.

Brandon lingered in the doorway for a moment, then walked slowly into the room. The expression on his face was one Jana hadn't seen before. She didn't know what it meant.

Brandon stopped near the desk and gazed down at her, looking troubled and unsure of himself.

"I think it's time you and I had a talk," Brandon said. "About the way things have been going around here."

Jana's hopes soared. Thank goodness. He was going to tell her to leave.

Chapter Ten

He would ask her to leave.

Jana's heart rate picked up as she contemplated the look on Brandon's face and guessed the reason for it. He was about to tell her that he'd been wrong. Their marriage just couldn't work. He wanted her to leave. Immediately.

A dozen ideas flashed in her mind. Dash out the front door. Ask Abbie to send her things. Rush to the hotel right away, collect her aunt and flee into the night. If they left immediately, they could reach San Francisco by morning. This whole nightmare would be behind her. She'd never have to see this house or Brandon again. Ever.

Ever?

An odd knot twisted Jana's stomach unexpectedly. Leave? Turn her back, walk away, never to return? Never finish decorating the house? Never learn how Mrs. Boone managed with the new recipes?

Never have Brandon kiss her again as he did outside her bedchamber?

Jana pushed aside those thoughts and mentally grabbed onto the recollections that had driven her from the house in the first place, the situations that still existed—and showed no signs of improving.

She rose from the chair and turned to face Brandon, ready to hear his decision, his edict that would set her free.

"Yes?" she asked, anxious suddenly to get this over with and, in fact, flee into the night.

"I think it would be a good idea if we…talked," Brandon told her, though he seemed to have a little difficulty getting the words out.

Had he lost his nerve? Now? When he was about to tell her the one thing she most wanted to hear from him?

A thread of anger found its way through Jana's swirling thoughts. He'd married her and treated her badly. He'd refused to grant her a divorce when she'd asked for it. He'd insisted they try to repair their marriage and had consumed several days of her life, causing her yet more heartache. Jana's irritation increased.

Yet Brandon still didn't speak. Instead, he moved away, paced to the settee, then turned back. He opened his mouth to speak, said nothing, then cleared his throat and finally spoke.

"I, ah, I wanted to tell you…"

"What?" Jana asked, a little more harshly than she'd intended.

Brandon seemed not to notice. He slid one hand into his trouser pocket, glanced at the floor, then at her again.

Say it, she thought. Say the words. Send her on her way.

"I wanted to tell you," he said, "that I'm very pleased with the way you've taken over the house."

"You're *what*?"

"Pleased," Brandon said again. He gestured, encompassing the house around them. "You've done a good job of resuming your duties."

"Oh."

"You've really taken hold of things around here," he said. "Just as we discussed."

Jana's hopes sank. So he wasn't going to ask her to leave, after all. Yet, for some reason, her stomach began to tingle in a strange new way.

Brandon paced to the side table across the room, then swung to face her. "And…and I wanted to tell you…something else."

Jana found herself at a complete loss now. She had no idea where this conversation was headed.

Brandon held his position a few yards away, as if needing the distance. He tilted his head right, then left, stretching the muscles of his neck. Jana steeled herself.

"I wanted to tell you," he said, "that while you were away I…missed you."

For an instant, Jana just stared. What had he said? That he missed her? Had she heard him correctly? Those words had actually been spoken by Brandon?

"Were you out in the heat too long today?" she asked.

"No," Brandon said quickly. He shifted his weight, as if wanting to move toward her but not allowing himself to budge from the spot where he'd planted himself. "I...I missed you."

Jana's surprise evaporated and in its place sprang a fountain of emotion. "You did?" she asked, taking a step toward him.

He nodded. "I did. And I...I thought of you...often."

Visions came to life in Jana's mind, scenes that Abbie had described of Brandon alone in her empty room touching her things, clutching her pillow. Jana's heart ached at the pain her departure and absence had caused him. She fought the urge to run to him, throw her arms around him.

"And," Brandon said, drawing in a fresh breath as if warming to his subject. "And I wanted to ask you why...exactly...you left me. I thought I knew the reason, but I decided that perhaps I was wrong."

"Really?"

"It occurred to me that some of the reasons you left might still trouble you, might keep you from being happy here," Brandon said. "I decided that I should ask you. I really hope you'll tell me."

Yes, of course she'd tell him. Jana's heart tumbled. She'd open the vault of woes she'd kept locked and tell him, tell him everything, explain how she'd felt, how hurt she'd been, how difficult a decision it had been to leave in the first place. He'd asked—he'd finally asked. After all those months in Europe when she hadn't heard a word from him, thought he didn't possibly care about her, wasn't interested in her, now he wanted to know *why*. He'd changed. Brandon had actually changed. Things would finally be good between them.

Based on what?

The cold voice of reason stopped Jana in her tracks just as she was about to dash across the room and throw herself into Brandon's arms.

Had he changed? Really? What evidence was there, aside from this one question he'd just posed?

During their courtship Brandon seemed as if he would be the perfect husband. After the marriage, snuggled in her bed together, he'd been wonderful.

But all along, he'd been someone entirely different. Someone whom Jana didn't like.

Had he truly changed now? How was that possible? Simply because he'd suddenly given her a compliment, confessed that he'd missed her and asked her for an explanation, did that mean he was different? That things would be different?

Perhaps.

But was it enough on which to base her entire future?

No. No, it wasn't. And the realization crashed down on Jana as if the very ceiling above her head had collapsed.

"So you want me to tell you why I left?" she asked.

Brandon nodded. "Yes, I do."

"Well, let's see," Jana mused. "There were so many reasons. Where do I start? Chronologically? Alphabetically? Categorically? Randomly? Which would you prefer?"

A guarded look crept over Brandon's features. "As you please."

Jana drew herself up, hardening her heart. She knew she sounded sarcastic and insensitive. But if she was ever going to leave this place, she'd have to squelch any hope of a reconciliation. On Brandon's part, as well as hers.

Because no matter what happened, she couldn't stay.

"I'm not going to tell you," she declared.

A few seconds passed, then Brandon's brows drew together. "You're not going to tell me?"

"No. I have no desire to explain myself to you."

"But that's not fair," Brandon told her, stepping closer. "You're using those facts against me—first to leave, and now to harbor ill feelings toward me. Yet you won't tell me what they are so I can change them."

His logic was perfect, of course, which only irritated Jana further.

She flung out her hand. "Yes, well, that's simply the way it is." Jana headed for the door.

"No."

Brandon's voice stopped her. He sounded hurt and outraged and confused. Jana turned and saw that his expression mirrored his tone.

"You said you'd try to make our marriage work," he told her. "You promised."

"But it's *not* working," she told him. Jana drew herself up, reaching deep inside for another dose of courage. "I want you to release me from my promise, Brandon. I want you to let me leave. Now."

Brandon shook his head. "No."

"Surely you can see we can't save our marriage."

"I don't see that at all," he insisted.

"You can find somebody new."

"I don't want to find anybody new."

"You can love someone else," Jana told him.

"No," Brandon said, his expression hardening.

Jana's shoulders sagged and she sighed heavily. "Brandon, please..."

"There was *something* you liked about our marriage, Jana. There had to be," Brandon said. "What about the way we used to walk through the garden in the evening? Remember? We'd stroll the grounds and talk about the plants. You liked that, didn't you?"

"No," she said and turned her head away.

"Why are you being so coldhearted?" Brandon asked, a genuine question, not an accusation. "Why? Why did you marry me when you...when you didn't love me?"

Jana reeled as if she'd been slapped. She straightened her shoulders and gazed directly into his eyes.

"I never said I didn't love you, Brandon."

She turned and left the room.

"Why can't I be more like you fellows?"

The two fat ducks offered Brandon no reply to his question as they plied the water, gliding along the lake's smooth surface. On weekends, Westlake Park teemed with people come to hear the musical performances in the band shell, ride the boats or picnic beneath the trees. But today, Brandon had the place mostly to himself.

Which was for the best, he realized, given that he was attempting to have a conversation with two ducks.

He sat back on the wooden bench near the shoreline and helped himself to a handful of popcorn he'd bought from a vendor. A solitary rowboat took to the water and several children scampered among the trees across the lake. The sky had darkened to a dull gray, yet rain didn't seem likely. A pleasant day, Brandon decided.

Yet he envied the ducks.

No problems. No troubles. Nothing for them to want, need or desire except food and shelter.

No business to run. No people standing by awaiting decisions.

No wife.

No heart to break.

Brandon sat forward bracing his elbows on his knees and tossed popcorn onto the water. The two ducks quacked and paddled over, scooping it up in their bills.

After last night and his discussion with Jana, he'd gone to his office this morning with the intention of shutting out the whole matter and catching up on several things he'd let slide these past few days. But he couldn't concentrate, so he had left his office and came to the lake. He liked it here, especially on weekdays when it was quiet. It was a good place to think.

And Brandon had a great deal of thinking to do.

He tossed more popcorn onto the water, a little farther out this time, and it attracted the attention of three other ducks. They honked and swam over.

He supposed he should have been hurt by Jana's actions last night. Her apparent disregard for his attempt to share his feelings with her, her blatant refusal to tell him why, exactly, she left him in the first place and give him a blueprint, of sorts, on how to improve himself for her should have crushed him. He wasn't given to displays of emotion. He knew that.

But he wasn't hurt. Not really. Because Jana had told him, in a roundabout way, that she loved him.

Brandon sat back on the bench feeling considerably lighter today than at any time in the past fourteen months. Jana loved him. Still. After all that had happened, she loved him.

And if she loved him, other problems could be overcome. He'd just have to figure out how.

Since Jana herself was offering no clue, even after his emotional outpouring last night, Brandon would have to uncover the reasons himself.

He sank a little lower on the bench, mentally toying with some possibilities of where their troubles might lie.

Could it have been his lovemaking?

No, of course not. What a preposterous idea. Brandon banished the thought from his mind.

Was he too rigid in his wants? Home by six, only certain meals, specific menus. Seldom any guests. Had he been too insistent on having things his own way? Ignored what Jana wanted?

She'd never said anything, but she'd been a little timid back then—nothing like the woman who had returned to him from Europe.

Should he have noticed that? What else was right in front of him that he'd not picked up on?

Rising from the bench, Brandon walked to the shoreline and flung the last of the popcorn onto the water. The ducks quacked and honked, swimming quickly and jockeying to scoop up the kernels.

Brandon closed his fist around the bag, giving in to the cold ache that had long lurked in the corners of his heart. His chest tightened with determination.

He wouldn't let Jana leave. Not again. He couldn't bear it. He couldn't survive it another time. He would find a way to make her stay.

Hardly an impossible situation. Brandon drew in a deep breath willing away the old pain, finding solace in the formulation of a plan, as he always did.

He'd built an empire of railroads, manufacturing, real estate and agriculture with little help from anyone. Surely he could figure out how to make one woman happy.

How hard could it be?

Chapter Eleven

Leona Albright wanted to see her? Regarding a "highly confidential and deeply personal matter"?

As the carriage swayed, carrying her through the streets of Los Angeles, Jana glanced down at the handwritten note that had been delivered to the house first thing this morning. She wished she could console herself with the notion that she had no idea what Leona Albright intended to tell her today. But, really, she thought she knew.

There was something between Leona and Brandon. Upon first meeting the woman shortly after arriving in Los Angeles as Brandon's new bride, Jana had sensed it. Yet she didn't know what it was, exactly.

Initially, she suspected a love affair between the two of them. Though Leona was more than ten years older than Brandon and hardly seemed his type, Jana had considered the possibility. But after seeing them together on several occasions, she came to doubt that anything of so intimate a nature had gone on between them.

Had she been wrong?

Jana slid Leona's luncheon invitation into her handbag and turned her attention to the passing scenery. It seemed that the woman was ready to confess all at their meeting today. Perhaps Jana would finally learn the truth. She'd be glad to know, finally. Yet her heart ached a little imagining what the "highly confidential and deeply personal matter" might be. She could think that it meant only one thing.

Jana shifted on the seat. Perhaps it would be for the best if Leona confessed an intimacy with Brandon. Certainly it was a just reason to leave him. One even Brandon couldn't attempt to deny.

Yet if the matter Leona wanted to discuss today proved to be something entirely different, Jana would have no choice but to stay with Brandon for the month, as she had promised. She'd asked him twice now to release her and he'd refused both times. What could she do but stay?

The carriage drew to a stop in front of Blossoms Restaurant, and the doorman assisted Jana to the sidewalk. The maître d' nodded respectfully when she walked inside.

"Your party will arrive shortly, Mrs. Sayer," he said. "Please come this way."

Jana had never been to this restaurant before and was surprised to be recognized. Establishments such as this catered to the wealthy and powerful, and they made it their business to know their patrons on sight. Yet how could they know her?

Conversation hummed low among the well-dressed diners as Jana followed the maître d' through the tables to the rear of the restaurant and down a short hallway to a smaller dining room. He seated her at a table set for two, bowed slightly and departed, leaving Jana totally alone in the room. Not one single diner was present, save herself.

But what a lovely place it was, Jana thought. The small octagonal-shaped room featured floor-to-ceiling windows on all but one side. Outside, a private garden tucked into a courtyard bloomed with a profusion of colorful flowers, lush shrubs and vines, and palms. The theme carried indoors with pale green linens, floral china, potted palms and fresh cuttings on every table.

Late-afternoon shadows dimmed the garden reminding Jana of the hour. She hoped Leona wouldn't keep her waiting. It was after four o'clock already and Jana had to be home before six.

A waiter appeared, poured water in the crystal goblet, then departed with nothing more than a bow and a faint smile. Jana fidgeted, wishing she'd insisted the maître d' seat her facing the door rather than the garden so she could see Leona's approach. Would the look on the woman's face foretell the purpose of today's surprise luncheon?

Jana told herself once again that she had no reason

to fear this meeting. If Leona told her the worst, Jana should, in fact, be glad to hear it.

Yet Jana could find no joy in that hypothetical situation. And now that the possibility of facing it was upon her...

Jana pressed her lips together, willing Leona Albright into the room.

Instead, a waiter appeared and offered a pleasant smile as he lit the small candle nestled among the table's floral centerpiece. He moved on to light the other candles in the wall and floor sconces around the room, then disappeared only to be replaced by a musician. With a brief bow to Jana, he stationed himself in a far corner, tucked a violin under his chin and began to play.

If this wasn't the strangest luncheon, Jana couldn't imagine what would be. Good gracious, what was Leona Albright thinking? Did she believe this oddly romantic setting would somehow soften the blow of revealing that she and Brandon had been—

A warm rush swept up Jana's neck, setting her nerves on end just as a hand reached around and lay a solitary rose beside her plate.

Brandon.

She turned to find him standing over her, looking especially dapper in a black suit and maroon necktie.

"What on earth are you—"

He cut her off by taking her hand gently in his. "Please forgive my impertinence at arranging this luncheon. I prevailed upon a mutual friend to lure you here under false pretenses. I'm Brandon Sayer."

"But Brandon—"

"More than anything, I'd like to get to know you," he continued. "Would you allow me that honor?"

Jana's heart fluttered wildly as the meaning of his charade dawned on her. A clandestine meeting, a plea to get to know her. He wanted them to start over.

Brandon placed his palm atop her hand, holding it just a trifle more firmly, and leaned down just a little. He gazed into her eyes. "Please?"

She couldn't deny him. She didn't *want* to deny him. Yet she knew she should. Knew it was for the best. But gazing into his eyes while her heart beat wildly, Jana couldn't bring herself to say the words.

Maybe she could stay. Maybe things would work out. The notion flew through her mind. He might have changed—truly changed. Perhaps they could make things work—even after all that had happened.

Even after what had happened in London.

"Yes, please," Jana said, surprised to hear how soft her own voice sounded. "Please, sit down."

Brandon took the chair across the little round table from her, bringing on a flurry of waiters. Napkins unfurled, champagne poured.

"This is a lovely restaurant," Jana said, glancing around. With the fading sunlight, the flickering candles reflected off the windows giving the room a romantic sparkle. "I'm surprised no one else is here—"

She stopped, and from the look on Brandon's face, realized what he'd done.

"You secured this entire room," she said. "Just for us."

"I wanted your full attention." The corner of his mouth lifted ever so slightly. "Selfish, yes. But worth it."

"And you enlisted the aid of Leona Albright in this bit of subterfuge?"

"I did."

"Likely, you also put off a number of business meetings and a great deal of work to be here."

Brandon nodded. "Everything else can wait."

"You went to a lot of trouble."

"You're nothing but trouble, Jana," he told her with a crooked twist to his lips.

She giggled at his honesty. "And you're sure you want to put up with that?"

The playful smile left his face. "I've never been more sure of anything in my life."

She fingered the single yellow rose he'd placed beside her plate. "My favorite."

"You had those in your hands when you walked down the aisle at our wedding," Brandon said. "Some blue flowers too. They matched the color of your eyes. There were small white flowers also."

"You remember?" she asked, genuinely pleased.

Brandon gazed across the table at her. "I remember everything."

The waiter served the soup and Jana expected their conversation to end. Brandon normally used the solitude of mealtime to think. So she was surprised when he spoke.

"What did you do today?" he asked.

He looked a bit uncomfortable asking the question. She could see that he was trying hard to do and say the right things.

Yet she didn't want to tell him that she'd spent a portion of the day at her aunt's hotel suite. He still didn't seem to know that Aunt Maureen was in town and she preferred to keep it that way.

"The usual," Jana said, sipping her soup. "Answering correspondence. We must be the most requested couple at social functions these days."

"How about the renovations?" Brandon asked, finishing his soup.

"Coming along nicely," Jana told him.

They finished supper, then lingered over dessert and coffee. Jana could see it was an effort for him. Brandon wasn't one to sit with no real purpose, to make idle conversation. Yet he did just that.

When they returned home, Brandon walked upstairs with her and paused outside the door to her bedchamber. Jana's skin heated, remembering the last time they'd stood here together, how he'd taken her in his arms, kissed her.

"Good night," Brandon said softly.

Would he do the same now? Tonight, after their romantic supper? It seemed the most natural thing in the world.

"Thank you for such a lovely evening," Jana said and felt herself sway toward him ever so slightly.

He eased closer, dropping his gaze to her lips for an instant. "I'm glad you liked it."

"I did," she said quickly.

A long moment passed with the two of them facing each other in the hallway of the silent house. Jana felt the heat of Brandon's body, saw the way his lower lip twitched, signs that she remembered.

He was about to kiss her. She knew it. Jana's heart thumped a little harder in her chest.

But instead, Brandon gulped in a breath and backed up a step. "Well…good night."

A wave of disappointment washed through Jana. "Good night," she replied.

Brandon turned away. She did the same.

"Jana?"

She whirled toward him again. "Yes?"

"If you'd care to join me for breakfast in the morning, I'd be pleased to have your company."

His words spoke of tomorrow, but his thoughts—so obvious from his expression—remained on tonight, Jana realized. But was she any better? Good gracious, she wanted nothing more than to divorce this man, yet here she stood hoping he'd kiss her.

She consoled herself with the thought that their lovemaking had never been a problem between them.

"I'd like that," Jana said.

Brandon nodded, then lingered when he could have headed off to his own bedchamber.

"Well, good night," he said. "Again."

"Good night."

They watched each other, then finally Brandon turned and walked down the hallway. Jana enjoyed one last look at him, then went into her own room.

Her gaze went immediately to the bed, Brandon still fully in her thoughts. The nights they'd spent here together, the mornings…

Jana gave herself a mental shake and headed for her dressing room. Enough of those sorts of thoughts. She had bigger problems and commitments than those under this roof. Yet she was obligated to stay.

Jana drew in a breath. She'd have to steel her feelings against Brandon. Somehow.

"Good morning," Jana said as she walked into the breakfast room.

Brandon, already seated at the table, looked up and came to his feet. He didn't smile, though, and Jana wondered at the wisdom of her decision to join him for breakfast, even after he'd invited her. This early hour— anywhere but in the bedroom—had always been a difficult time for them.

"Morning," he said, and pulled out the chair to his right.

He seated her, then resumed his own spot and turned his attention to the two morning newspapers spread out before him. Jana waited while the servant poured coffee and took away Brandon's empty plate, then sipped and listened to the ticking of the hallway clock, her most reliable companion in the house.

Just when she was about to excuse herself and go upstairs again, Brandon jumped, giving her a start, and turned to her quickly.

"Sorry," he said, as if just remembering he was supposed to be paying attention to her.

"How is the *Messenger* this morning?" she asked, gesturing toward the newspaper.

"Dull as ever," Brandon said, pushing it away. "And costing me a fortune."

"Oliver Fisk seems like such a nice man," Jana said.

"'Nice' doesn't make money," Brandon said, sipping his coffee.

"What are your plans for the day?" Jana asked.

"Nothing out of the ordinary," Brandon said, lifting the coffee cup to his lips again. He paused, as if reminding himself that a more detailed response was called for, then lowered it to the saucer. "I'm having a meeting this morning with several business owners from Pasadena. They're looking for office space here in the city."

"Is this about your Jennings project?"

"Yes. Word of it has spread. The building is filling up quickly," Brandon said.

"Do you think that's wise?" Jana asked. "Committing rental space in the building when the newspaper is still there?"

"The *Messenger* is a lost cause," Brandon said.

"But if Oliver somehow manages to revive it, won't that put you in a difficult position?"

"*If* it should happen, yes." He shook his head. "But it won't."

Jana just looked at him, realizing this was the most information about his workday he'd shared with her—ever. For a moment, she didn't know what to say, how to act.

"What?" Brandon looked uncomfortable, reacting, no doubt, to the odd look on her face.

"Nothing," Jana said.

"No, tell me. Did I say something wrong?" Brandon asked. "I thought you might really want to know what I was doing. If you don't, if it's not interesting, I—"

"It's fine," she told him. "I'm interested. I really am. It's just that you don't usually share that sort of information with me. It's just different, that's all."

He leaned toward her a bit. "Good different?"

She smiled. "Yes. Good different."

"Well, all right then." Brandon sighed heavily. "And what are you up to this morning?"

"I'll be here," Jana said. "There're a few things I want to discuss with the construction foreman."

Brandon's brows drew together. "You're not knocking out another wall, are you?"

She grinned. "Not today."

"I'd better go." Brandon got to his feet and assisted Jana from her chair.

"We're having supper tonight with the Carmichaels," Jana reminded him. "Don't forget."

"A supper with someone whose company I enjoy? How could I forget?" Brandon gave her a little grin and left.

* * *

A brisk knock sounded on Brandon's office door just as Noah Carmichael strode inside. Brandon crumpled the paper he'd been writing on and tossed it in the trash can, along with the dozen he'd already discarded.

Notes to himself, lists of things he should—and shouldn't—do. Ideas. Plans. All with the sole purpose of making Jana happy and getting her to stay. The whole process was mentally exhausting. One thing was certain: courting a fiancée had been a hell of a lot easier than winning the heart of his own wife.

"Are you still going to look at those warehouses this afternoon?" Noah asked, stopping in front of Brandon's desk. When he nodded Noah went on. "Want some company?"

"Sure."

Noah raised an eyebrow. "You're acting a little more agreeable today. Does this mean you and Jana are finally—"

"Shut up, Noah. It's none of your business."

"Ah, yes. There's the old Brandon Sayer we all know and love." Noah chuckled. "I saw your lovely bride a few minutes ago."

Brandon put down his pen and looked up at Noah. "This morning? Just now?"

He nodded. "She was going into the Morgan Hotel. I wanted to speak with her, be certain you two were coming to supper tonight, but she dashed inside before I caught up with her."

Brandon frowned. He was certain Jana had said she intended to remain at home this morning. Something to do with the construction crew, wasn't it? Yes, he was sure that was it.

He sat back in his chair. Why on earth would Jana go to the Morgan Hotel?

Chapter Twelve

The Carmichael home was located in Bunker Hill, a community of lovely mansions owned by some of the city's most important families. Jana watched out the carriage window as they pulled to a stop in front of the three-story gingerbread-trimmed home.

"I hope Beth won't be upset with us," she mused. They were late leaving home this evening, Jana oddly enough the first to be ready and waiting in the carriage for Brandon to join her.

"I doubt she will," Brandon said as he exited the carriage, then offered his hand and assisted Jana to the ground.

The house windows glowed a welcoming yellow as they climbed the steps to the wide, sweeping porch. The front door opened and Noah waved them inside.

She'd been a bit uncomfortable at the thought of visiting the Carmichaels tonight. She remembered meeting Beth during the first three months she'd lived in the city, and remembered her as one of the genuinely nice people she had met here. But she didn't know Noah as well and suspected that, as a staunch friend of Brandon's, he might harbor some ill feelings toward her for running out on their marriage.

But any such thoughts didn't present themselves as Noah took Jana's hand warmly. "It's so good to see you again," he told her.

Jana smiled and relaxed a little as she walked into the foyer and the men exchanged words and a handshake.

"Jana!"

Beth Carmichael swept toward them looking a bit flustered and harried, but wearing a bright smile. She wore a dark blue gown; tendrils of her brunette hair curled about her round face.

"Jana, I'm so glad you're here!" Beth took both of Jana's hands. "I told Noah he absolutely must deliver my invitation and see that you two came to supper immediately. I'm so glad you could come tonight."

Jana's heart warmed at her enthusiastic welcome and she couldn't help but smile in return. "Thank you so much for inviting us."

"Come into the parlor," Beth insisted, drawing Jana alongside her, leaving the men to follow.

Jana gazed around at the marble entryway, the tasteful furnishings. "Your home is lovely."

"Look, Jana," Brandon said. "They even have walls."

Jana smiled at his good-natured joke, but Beth looked confused.

"Jana has several renovation projects underway at home," Brandon explained. "I'm sure it will all turn out fine in the end, but right now, we're missing several walls."

Beth's eyes widened and she turned to Jana. "You knocked out walls?"

She nodded. "Yes, but then I decided to put them up again."

"Oh, my…" Beth pressed her lips together and gazed thoughtfully around the foyer. "Perhaps I should think about doing something like that."

"Not right now," Noah said and slipped his arm around his wife's shoulders. "I think the construction project you have underway now is quite enough."

Beth blushed and touched her palm to her belly. "Yes, I suppose so."

Jana gasped. "Are you…?"

Beth beamed. "Yes."

"Oh! How wonderful!" Jana couldn't resist giving Beth a hug. "Congratulations. I'm so happy for you."

Noah tilted his head. "Why is it *I* never get any of the credit for my significant contribution to the project?"

Beth's face flushed bright red and she swatted him on the arm. "Oh, hush."

"Have you started on the baby's room yet?" Jana asked.

"Would you like to see it?"

"Of course."

In the nursery on the second floor, Beth went into great detail about her plans for the suite. Under construction now, wallpaper rolls and paint cans cluttered the rooms along with sawhorses and tools left behind by the carpenters.

"I'm going to put this on the walls in here where the baby will sleep," Beth explained, holding up a sample of wallpaper. She flipped through the pattern book. "But in the playroom next door, I'm going to use this one."

Jana eyed the yellow ducks and fluffy lambs. "It's perfect."

Beth gestured toward the wall. "Then over there, I'm going to—"

"All right, all right, you don't have to finish this room tonight," Noah said as he and Brandon walked into the room. "Supper's ready."

Beth smiled up at him. "I'm just so excited."

He slid his arm around her waist and gazed down at her, love burning in his eyes. "Come have your supper. You have to keep up your strength."

"Yes, of course. Let's go eat." Beth left the room on her husband's arm, leaving Jana and Brandon in the half-finished nursery.

Yet the joy which the new life that was destined to occupy this room would bring to Beth and Noah was lost on Jana. Brandon, too, she thought. Standing alone in the room, the uncertainty of their own future was too much to bear. Jana saw the same in Brandon's expression.

"We'd better go," she said quietly.

Brandon nodded and they left the nursery together.

Supper was an informal affair, just the four of them, so the usual gathering in the parlor and procession to the dining room was unnecessary. They sat around the table that managed to seem cozy even with the china, crystal and fine linens.

"Jana, has Aurora Chalmers put you to work yet?" Beth asked, as the servants moved silently around the room. "Brandon, you know Mrs. Chalmers, don't you?"

"Yes. Unfortunately," he responded. "The woman who always wants her name in the newspaper."

Jana knew the woman well also, even after so brief a time in the city. Mrs. Chalmers headed up nearly every charitable function in Los Angeles, more out of a desire to see her name in print than from a devotion to worthy causes. Without a doubt, she was the grand dame of polite society, and her approval on a project was mandatory if it had any hope of succeeding.

"Actually," Jana said, "I've been invited to have tea with her later this week. I'm sure she'll want to assign me to some sort of charitable committee."

"You should work at the women's refuge," Beth said. "That's where I donate my time."

"But just for a while longer," Noah was quick to say. "You have to take it easy now."

Beth gave him a sweet smile.

"What's the women's refuge all about?" Jana asked.

"It was begun about a year ago by Amanda Hastings, Mrs. Nick Hastings. They're neighbors of yours," Beth said. "She started it as a shelter for women with children who have been abandoned by their husbands or left widowed."

"Sounds as if it's a very worthwhile cause," Jana said.

"Oh, it is," Beth agreed. "Amanda's done a marvelous job with it. There're rooms for the women and children to live in, and schooling for the women so they can find jobs. The refuge has a playroom for the children, an infirmary, a kitchen and dining room. Almost everything you can think of."

"Has Mrs. Hastings lost interest in the project?" Jana asked.

"Oh, no." Beth blushed another time. "She's expecting. Due in only a few weeks, I believe."

"So be careful if you decide to work there," Noah said with a devilish grin. "Every woman who goes in the place winds up in the family way."

Jana felt Brandon's hot gaze on her from across the table, but she turned away, unable to meet his eye.

They finished supper and Jana and Beth chatted in the parlor while the men went elsewhere.

"I wish you'd think about working at the women's refuge," Beth said. "I haven't been feeling well, with the baby on the way, and it's such a good cause. Will you think about it?"

Jana hesitated to commit. In her heart, she knew she wouldn't be in town for more than a month, so she didn't want to take on so much that she left a vacuum in the wake of her departure. Yet it was certainly a worthwhile cause, one she'd like to devote her time to.

"Yes," Jana said. "I'll think about it."

Soon after, they left the Carmichaels with thank-yous, hugs, and promises to get together again soon. On the carriage ride home, Brandon sat in the seat across from Jana, silent in the darkness. Had it been anyone else, she might have thought he'd dozed off. She knew Brandon better. He was probably thinking about business. But when the carriage passed beneath a gaslight and she caught a glimpse of him, she realized he was looking at her breasts.

He walked her to the door of her bedchamber, as he had the night before, then lingered, making her wonder if he'd kiss her again. All the talk tonight of babies seemed to have had an effect on him, though she couldn't say exactly what it was.

But at her door he simply told her good-night and walked down the hallway to his own bedchamber. Jana went inside her room, dropped her handbag on the bureau and took off her hat.

Something on her bed caught Jana's gaze. A single yellow rose on her pillow. A folded note card lay beside it.

Had Brandon left it for her? Was it the reason he'd been late coming to the carriage tonight? Had he slipped into her room and placed it on her bed so she'd find it when they returned?

Yet if it wasn't Brandon, who could it be? Jana hardly knew what to think.

She picked up the note card and saw Brandon's large, bold handwriting. Inside, he'd written: I want you in my life/For now and always/Forever my wife.

It was the worst poem she'd ever read, yet tears swelled in her eyes. Brandon had written her a poem. And left it with her favorite yellow rose.

Emotion tightened her throat. She turned toward the connecting door to his bedchamber, a door that had always been open between the rooms during the first three months of their marriage, yet remained closed tight since her return.

She should thank him for the rose, for the poem. Even though it was late and it could wait until morning, Jana wanted to do it now.

But opening their connecting door wasn't a step she was ready to take. Jana slipped into the hallway and down to his bedchamber. She knocked gently and the door opened so quickly she wondered if he'd been waiting for her arrival.

Brandon looked out at her, tall and handsome in the soft light. He'd taken off his jacket and necktie, and opened his shirt collar. Dark, coarse hair curled over the top of his shirt and she glimpsed a wedge of his white cotton undershirt. His chest beneath it was strong and hard, taut with muscles.

And why wasn't she sharing her bed with him now?

Jana pushed the thought from her head, fearful that it had shown in her expression.

"Thank you for the rose," she said, forcing her gaze onto his face, forbidding it to drop lower. "And the poem."

He shrugged as if a little embarrassed. "I'm not much of a poet."

"It was beautiful," she said, because, really, it was.

They stared at each other for a long moment. Jana couldn't think of anything else to say, yet didn't want to leave. Brandon seemed to be scouring his thoughts for a topic of conversation too.

Finally, he said, "Are you thinking of helping out at the women's refuge?"

"Do you think it would be all right?" she asked. A woman wouldn't consider taking on even volunteer work without the approval of her husband. Though Jana had lived apart from him for so long and made all her own decisions, asking Brandon seemed the right thing to do.

"You'd be perfect for it," Brandon told her. "They would be lucky to have you."

She smiled, pleased to hear him say he thought her competent. So different from the first three months of their marriage.

"Noah and Beth seemed happy about the baby," Brandon said. He drew in a breath. "I'd like for us to have a child together...when things straighten out."

Jana's breath caught. She glanced away. "Well, good night."

She turned and headed toward her bedchamber.

"Jana?"

She looked back. Brandon had stepped into the hallway and was watching her closely. She didn't know what to make of it.

"I meant to ask you," he said. "How did your meeting go with the construction foreman this morning?"

"Fine," she said. "He understands what I want and assured me things would be handled accordingly."

"Did your meeting last all morning?"

Jana's breath caught. "Most of the morning."

"I see." Brandon gazed at her for another long moment, then disappeared into his room.

Jana hesitated, her heart thumping harder, then hurried into her room and closed the door.

Chapter Thirteen

A simple luncheon. That's all it had been. Surely...

Brandon paced outside the doorway of the storage room off the kitchen that Jana had resigned him to while renovations continued on his study. He couldn't bring himself to go inside the tiny, airless room. Just as he couldn't go to his office downtown this morning, or even leave the house.

The situation he'd wrestled with since yesterday was too big.

When Noah had told him that he'd witnessed Jana going into the Morgan Hotel, Brandon had figured it was for a luncheon. Women did that sort of thing all the time. Luncheons, teas, social gatherings. It was how they spent their days, how they planned community functions and charitable events. Perfectly innocent.

Yet Brandon couldn't get off his mind what Noah had

said. He kept imagining the worst. Jana in an affair with another man. The thought sickened him.

He had no reason to doubt her. No proof, not even any evidence. Jana had always been faithful to him in the past.

But she had left him. And she'd never told him exactly what had gone on in Europe. She'd denied him his husbandly rights and barred him from her bedchamber.

Brandon rubbed his forehead. All he had to do was ask her. Confront her. Demand to know what, exactly, she'd been doing at the Morgan.

But if he asked her, would she interpret it as an accusation? If it wasn't true, would the implied insult be just the excuse she'd been looking for to leave him again?

Brandon's hand closed into a fist. If he asked and she confirmed it was true, he'd be forced to confront the man. That suited him fine. He'd wanted to hit something for a while now.

But he was only borrowing trouble. Brandon bit off a curse, knowing that he had nothing but his own suspicion and *that* he'd pulled out of the air. And didn't he have his hands full already just dealing with reality?

"Hell…"

Brandon snatched up his satchel from the corner of the little room and strode through the house to the sitting room that Jana always used. He found her on the settee surrounded by pattern books, balancing a tablet on her lap.

"Finished your work already?" she asked, gazing up at him.

He'd told her at breakfast this morning that he intended to work at home for a while this morning; she didn't seem to suspect that he'd been too suspicious of her actions to leave the house.

"I don't know how the hell you expect me to work in that broom closet you call a study," Brandon grumbled.

"So you're going to your office in town?"

Did she sound anxious? Hoping he would leave?

Brandon shook the thought from his head.

"No. I'm not leaving," he told her.

Brandon grasped the small writing desk in the corner and dragged it across the room to the window. Then he took a side table and pulled it alongside.

"Charles!" he bellowed. "Charles, get in here!"

Jana got to her feet. "Brandon, what on earth are you doing?"

"I'm working in here," he told her. "Charles!"

"In *here?* But you can't—"

"Yes, sir?" Charles dashed into the room, obviously as unaccustomed to hearing Brandon shout as Jana was.

"Go into my study and find my chair. My comfortable chair," Brandon said. "It's under all those shrouds, somewhere. And tell some of those workmen to bring it in here."

"Yes, sir," he answered, and hurried away.

"But, Brandon," Jana said, "you can't work in here."

He opened his satchel and unloaded the ledgers. "Why not?"

"Because *I'm* working in here." She gestured to the pattern books piled up around her.

"Don't worry," Brandon told her. "You won't disturb me."

"But—"

Charles hustled into the room again, taking great care to direct the two workmen who carried Brandon's chair. The butler cautioned them about bumping the other pieces of furniture, then had them place it just so behind the little writing desk.

"Will there be anything else, sir?" Charles asked, as the workmen left the room.

"No. That's all," he said. "Thank you."

Charles hurried away.

With a nod of satisfaction, Brandon took off his jacket and hung it on the back of his chair, then sat down.

"You're not actually going to work in here, are you?" Jana asked, walking over.

"Is there some reason you don't want me here?" he countered.

"Well, no, not really…I suppose."

A less than convincing response. Was there a reason for it? Brandon wondered again, then hated himself for his suspicion.

"What are you doing, anyway?" he asked, gesturing to the wallpaper sample books on the settee.

"Several of the guest bedchambers upstairs have yet to be decorated," Jana explained.

Brandon shrugged. The doors to all the rooms upstairs remained closed, except for his and Jana's now that she'd returned. He knew furniture had been selected for the rooms and moved into them fourteen months ago, but hadn't bothered to notice what else still needed to be accomplished.

"I want to finish the rooms," Jana said.

"All of them?" Brandon asked. The suite of rooms on the back of the house flashed into his mind. The nursery. Empty, now. Always to be that way?

Last night at supper Noah and Beth Carmichael had certainly seemed happy with each other, with their lives and their upcoming arrival. Would he and Jana ever find that same happiness? Could he figure out the key to making Jana stay with him before these four weeks were up?

Right now, she didn't even seem to want him working in the same room with him.

"Excuse me, madam," Charles's voice intoned from across the room. "You have a visitor. Mr. McDowell."

A little wave of guilt washed through Brandon. He'd been suspicious of Jana's motives today, and all along she'd been waiting here for the decorator to arrive and continue the work on the upstairs rooms. Work Brandon had insisted was her duty and responsibility upon her return.

Feeling a little ashamed of himself, Brandon unloaded the rest of his things from his satchel as Jana left the room. He settled behind the desk and opened one of the ledgers. Minutes ticked by.

He expected them to return here to look over the wallpaper samples. Where were they? Brandon drummed his fingers on the desk, then closed the ledger and went to find them.

Voices drew him to the drawing room just down the hall from the foyer, a place where guests were customarily received. The tone of the conversation he overheard as he approached caused Brandon to stop outside the doorway. He leaned in a little, just enough to see Jana and Mr. McDowell standing in the center of the room.

"As I've already told you," Jana said, "I did not ask you to come over today, Mr. McDowell. Your services are not needed."

"But *of course* they are," the man answered.

McDowell's dress was impeccable, his hair slicked carefully in place, his mustache waxed to perfection. He'd come highly recommended when Brandon had begun construction on the house. Yet there was something about the man that never sat quite right with Brandon.

"Your husband advised me of your *return*," McDowell said, "He instructed me to come here to see to the *rest* of the decorating. I've been here several times *already,* Mrs. Sayer, and frankly I'm a bit irked by your refusal to let me get on with my work. It's only your *husband's* reputation that keeps me from abandoning you completely."

Jana drew herself up. "Once again, Mr. McDowell, let me say that I do not require any assistance on your part. I am perfectly capable—"

"Oh, *really*." McDowell laughed, touching a hand to his chest. "How sweet, my dear girl, that you think you can attempt to take on a project of this nature. It's price-less, really."

"Mr. McDowell—"

"Stand aside, dear. I have a *great* deal to do and I doubt your husband would approve of you wasting my time with your *delusions,*" McDowell said, brushing past Jana.

Anger flared in Brandon. Only a little earlier today he'd wanted to hit something. Now seemed like the perfect time.

"What's going on here?" he demanded, striding into the room.

"Mr. Sayer," McDowell crooned, sounding relieved to see him. He waved his hand in the general direction of Jana. "This dear little wife of yours is in need of a good *talking to* on your part, if you don't mind my saying so."

Brandon glanced at Jana. Her back was rigid, her jaw set, her mouth pressed in a thin line. This certainly wasn't the timid, naive bride he'd married. This was a grown woman, one who knew exactly what she wanted. Where had Jana gotten this determined streak?

And why did he find it so appealing? Brandon wanted her, right there on the spot.

"Now," McDowell said, "if you'll come with me, Mr. Sayer, we can go over all the work that remains to be done."

"*Mr. McDowell.*" Jana flung the words across the room. "I have already told you your services are not required."

The decorator didn't bother to turn and look at her. Instead, he gave her words a dismissive shrug and said to Brandon, "Shall we proceed?"

Was this the sort of thing Jana had to deal with when McDowell had been working on the house before? Brandon wondered. Had he been this condescending, this rude to her?

Jana's confrontation with the cook a few days ago came to mind. Mrs. Boone had been just as disrespectful to her. Had Jana's wishes been completely disregarded by her also?

Brandon looked at McDowell. The man's brows rose, as if he was wondering what was taking so long. Then Brandon turned his gaze on Jana. She didn't move. Just stood rigid. Waiting.

Brandon turned to McDowell. "You're fired."

"What?" His face reddened and his cheeks puffed out like a toad. "I—but—you—"

"If my wife says your services aren't needed," Brandon told him, "then they're not needed."

"Well!" McDowell drew himself up, then stuck out his chin and left the room in a huff.

Brandon walked over to where Jana stood. "Is that the sort of thing you had to put up with when he was doing the decorating before?"

"Yes," she said, finally relaxing her stance a bit.

"Why didn't you tell me?" he asked.

She shrugged. "You were gone, busy all the time, and…well, I didn't really know how to tell you."

"I'm sorry," Brandon said softly.

She gave him a weak smile.

"Would you like me to fire Mrs. Boone also?" he asked.

Jana's smile widened, and it pleased Brandon to no end that he'd elicited it from her.

"No, that won't be necessary," Jana said. "Mrs. Boone and I are learning to get along."

"Hire whomever you want to help with the decorating," Brandon said. "Or handle it yourself. You're doing a fine job of it. I'm sure my yellow study will turn out well."

"Actually," Jana said. "I was thinking of changing the color from yellow to something else."

"Really?"

"How do you feel about lilac?"

Brandon looked at her. "Lilac will be perfect."

Jana smiled. "Thank you for understanding about Mr. McDowell."

"If you change your mind about me firing Mrs. Boone, just say so," he offered. "Or any of the rest of the staff…or the entire staff. Whatever you want, Jana."

"Thank you." She laughed gently and walked away.

"Jana?"

She turned back.

"Were you involved with another man while you were in London?"

The stunned expression on her face caused Brandon's stomach to knot.

"Were you?" he asked.

Jana shook her head. "No."

"In Europe?"

"No."

Brandon steeled himself. "And since your return?"

A wry smile quirked her lips. "After our three months of marriage, believe me, the very *last* thing I wanted was another man in my life."

That he believed.

"Fine, then," he said, then felt guilty for his suspicion. "I'm sorry to ask, but—"

"It's all right," Jana said. "We were apart for a long time. And married for a very short time. I'm sure there's a great deal we don't know about each other."

Brandon nodded. Jana left the room and he stood there thinking about what she'd said.

And what she hadn't said.

When he'd asked her about an involvement since her return to Los Angeles, she hadn't given him an answer at all.

Chapter Fourteen

"Well, what do you think?" Beth asked.

Jana nodded her approval as they walked down the hallway of the women's refuge Beth had told her about at supper nearly a week ago. They'd just finished a tour of the facility and Jana was pleased to see that every room was spotless, every child and every mother clean and well fed.

"It's a very worthwhile cause," Jana said as she followed Beth into the office near the front entrance. "But it must take a great deal of work to keep it running smoothly."

"Not really. The women in residence do most of the work themselves." Beth gestured to the slate board on the wall where a grid of duties and volunteers had been written in chalk. "The women and older children gladly take on many of the duties here. Most of them have suffered some hard times before arriving."

Jana could well imagine the difficulties these women faced. Abandoned or widowed, left with children to provide for, most women lacked the skills and training to find jobs, to feed and clothe their families. Many were forced to accept charity from a kind relative, and if that wasn't forthcoming, farm out their children to whomever would take them, or leave them at an orphanage.

Jana shuddered at the thought.

"Do the women resent the ladies who volunteer?" Jana asked. "I mean, women such as those in our social circle. We have so much and they are barely getting by."

"Quite the opposite," Beth told her. "In fact, the women in residence here seem very interested in the things we can teach them. They ask questions about etiquette, manners, proper table settings, how to write a thank-you note. Anything to better themselves."

"Really?" Jana asked, a little surprised. "You and I take that sort of thing for granted. We've been schooled in proper etiquette our whole lives, attended classes, read books on the subject. The women here probably never had access to that sort of information."

"We've incorporated some of those things into classes and, so far, it's been very well received," Beth said. "And, of course, the women help each other with all sorts of things. Problems with relatives, children who misbehave, friends who turned their backs on them in times of need."

Jana smiled. "Those sort of problems know no bounds. We're all dealing with that kind of thing."

"The most difficult volunteer posts to fill are tutors willing to come in and work with the women on subjects such as math and English."

She pointed to another chart on the board and Jana saw many empty slots. "Everyone is eager to donate their money," Beth said, "but not their time and expertise. You'd have to coax volunteers."

"What about the refuge's finances?" Jana asked, glancing at a stack of ledgers on the edge of the desk.

"There's an accounting firm that handles the money, and a trustee who oversees the accountants. All we have to do is place orders for groceries and supplies, then keep the records so they can be reviewed monthly," Beth explained. "For large expenditures, we simply write up a proposal and present it to the trustee for consideration."

"Sounds simple enough," Jana said.

"It is," Beth agreed. "But you'll only need to concern yourself with finding volunteer tutors. That will be your responsibility here—if you decide to help out."

Jana looked again at the vacant spots on the volunteer board. "The hardest job of all will be mine, huh?"

"Sometimes a fresh face and a new approach works wonders," Beth told her. "So, what do you—"

"Beth?" A young woman stepped into the office, then stopped short when she saw Jana. "Oh, sorry."

"It's fine," Beth said, waving her into the room. "Come in, Audrey. I'd like you to meet Jana Sayer. Jana, this is my cousin Audrey Bishop."

"Pleased to meet you," Audrey said, favoring her with a bright smile.

She was a pretty girl, probably no more than eighteen years old, petite, slender with dark hair and stunning green eyes, and a smile that lit up the room. Her dress was a pink confection of ruffles and flounces, just the sort of thing Jana had worn only a few years ago.

"Audrey lives near San Bernardino," Beth explained. "Her father owns orange groves there."

"A boring farm," Audrey said, wrinkling her nose. "Beth and Noah are good enough to let me come for a long visit from time to time."

"Do you help out here at the shelter?" Jana asked.

"I love helping out, especially with the babies," Audrey said.

"I brought Audrey here initially so she could see the importance of marrying well," Beth said, then shook her head. "But she sees it differently."

"Marry well?" Audrey repeated, dismissing the idea with a wave of her hand. "Seems to me it's more important for a woman to get an education and learn to fend for herself."

Jana smiled. How could she disagree? And how could she turn her back on such a worthwhile cause?

"You've convinced me," she said to Beth. "I'll take over the volunteer search, get people in here to teach English and math, and whatever else is needed."

"Wonderful," Beth said. She sighed. "What a relief."

The bell over the door at the front entrance

clanged. Audrey leaned out of the office and her eyes widened.

"Now here's something we don't often see at the shelter," she said, her brows lifting. "A man."

A few seconds later, Brandon appeared in the office doorway. Jana gasped at seeing him, and her heart beat a little faster. How could he still have that effect on her?

"Afternoon, ladies," he said, taking off his bowler and nodding to them.

"Brandon, this is a surprise," Jana said, but really it wasn't. Lately, he'd made a point of asking her every morning at breakfast about her plans for the day. At first she thought it odd, then he started dropping by at luncheons bringing her flowers or having a poem delivered along with a single yellow rose. He'd made her the talk—and the envy—of all her friends.

"Just thought I'd stop by," Brandon said, "and take a look at where my donations have been going."

"To a very worthy cause," Jana said, "from everything I see here."

"Jana's offered to volunteer for us," Beth said, then added, "If that's all right with you, of course."

Brandon nodded. "Whatever Jana wants is fine with me."

"Would you like a tour?" Beth offered.

"From your newest volunteer?" Brandon asked, looking at Jana. "Of course."

"My duties have begun," Jana said with a laugh as she led the way out of the office.

As she walked at Brandon's side down the hallway, Jana couldn't help but think how out of place he looked here. Tall, strong, sturdy, he seemed too big, too masculine for this place that catered to women and children.

He attracted attention. Wherever they went in the shelter, every child, every woman stopped what they were doing and looked up. If Brandon noticed that he was the center of attention, he didn't remark on it or react. Rather, he seemed enthralled with every word Jana spoke about the place.

"So, what we need most," she said, as they stepped out onto the back porch overlooking the rear yard, "is tutors for things like English and math."

Brandon tilted his head. "Seems to me what you need is a few men around this place."

So he had noticed. "I think perhaps some of the women here haven't had positive experiences with their husbands," Jana said.

"But what about the kids?" Brandon gestured to the yard where about two dozen children played. They'd segregated themselves, the younger ones playing in a sandbox, a group of girls jumping rope, and at the back of the yard, older boys kicking a ball back and forth between them.

"Those boys," he said. "They need a man around. Not a bunch of women."

"Are you volunteering?" Jana asked.

"Not to teach math or English," he told her.

"That's all right," Jana said. "I think I know how to solve that problem."

"You're sure about this, Mrs. Sayer? You're really sure?"

"Yes, Oliver," Jana said as she and the young newspaper editor walked through the front entrance of the women's refuge. "You'll be fine."

"I don't know…." Oliver adjusted his round spectacles, settling them more comfortably on his nose. "I've never actually taught anything before, and I'm not certain that I have the knack for it. In fact, I might do more harm than good here."

When she'd agreed to take on the task of finding volunteers, Jana had thought immediately that Oliver Fisk was the perfect person to help the women improve their reading and writing skills. She'd made a trip to his office at the *Messenger* and presented her case. Oliver had been so flustered at seeing her there he'd spilled his coffee and knocked a stack of papers into the floor, but had agreed to her request right away. Now it seemed he was having second thoughts.

"You'll be fine," Jana told him. "You're perfect to help the women with their English. I can't imagine anyone more qualified."

"Well, all right," Oliver said, passing his satchel from one hand to the other. "If you say so."

"Come inside. Let's get you settled."

She led the way into the office and saw Audrey filling in a space on the volunteer board.

"How did the math tutoring go?" Jana asked.

"Fine. Mrs. Monterey seems a natural," Audrey said, then dropped the chalk and turned around. "She's coming back next—"

Audrey stopped still at the sight of Oliver Fisk trailing Jana into the office. But this wasn't the same surprised look Jana had seen on the girl's face when Brandon had walked into the refuge. This was something else entirely.

Jana glanced at Oliver. He seemed frozen on the spot, his gaze locked on Audrey. Jana made introductions.

"I'm pleased to meet you, Mr. Fisk," Audrey said, her voice a breathy little sigh.

Oliver opened his mouth but only a few stuttered words managed to escape.

"Oliver will be helping the ladies with their English today," Jana said, as she unpinned her hat and placed it on the corner cabinet. "Perhaps you could show him the classroom?"

"Certainly. This way please," Audrey said, leading the way out of the office.

Oliver, clasping the handle of his satchel in front of his chest with both hands, didn't move. He didn't seem to be breathing, either.

Jana tried to hold back her grin as she gave him a little nudge. "It's all right, Oliver. Run along."

Yet another moment passed before the words seemed

to sink in. Finally, he turned and joined Audrey waiting in the hallway.

She looked back inside at Jana. "Oh, by the way, do you know about what's going on in the backyard?"

Jana frowned. "What is it?"

Audrey gave her a devilish smile. "If I were you, I'd get back there right away."

Good gracious, what was happening? She couldn't imagine.

Jana hurried down the hallway, past Audrey and Oliver still clutching his satchel and walking like a wooden toy soldier. She opened the back door and stepped outside.

The afternoon sun shone bright overhead in the blue, cloudless sky. A high wooden fence surrounded the large play yard, separating it from the alley out back and the building on either side. School had been dismissed for the day, so the older children now filled the yard, running in the grass, playing beneath the three towering oaks.

Nothing seemed amiss, Jana thought as she took in the yard and the children, until her gaze fell on a group of boys huddled together under the trees near the back fence, all sorts of boards and tools around them. She wondered what they were up to. Perhaps she should find out.

Jana passed a group of girls jumping rope and several more playing tag as she crossed the yard, then jerked to a halt.

Brandon.

Her breath caught. Standing amid the boys, he looked taller, stronger than usual. He had on brown work trousers and boots. The pale blue work shirt stood open part of the way down his chest, revealing his cotton undershirt that clung to every muscle. The sleeves were rolled back to his elbows, displaying his forearms covered with coarse hair.

Jana's knees weakened. When she'd left him it *hadn't* been because of his looks. Even now she still wasn't immune to his masculinity.

She must look as smitten as Oliver Fisk had a few minutes ago, Jana realized. Should she run back to the refuge before Brandon saw her?

She glanced back at the building and was stunned to see women standing at every window on both floors, gazing out. At Brandon.

So this was what Audrey was referring to when she'd told Jana to come out here. A odd tremor passed through Jana. She certainly wasn't going back inside now.

Smoothing a lock of hair in place, Jana headed over to where Brandon and the boys worked. He saw her and walked to join her.

"What are you doing?" she asked, feeling the urge to stand in front of him, block the view of all the women leering at her husband.

"Working," he said, giving her a hearty smile.

The work did seem to agree with him. Perspiration dampened his brow. The breeze had blown his hair over his forehead and she had a sudden urge to run her fingers through it.

"We're building a tree house," Brandon said, nodding toward the boys.

"But—but I didn't realize you knew how to do this sort of thing," Jana blurted out. She didn't even know he owned work clothes.

Brandon grinned and eased a little closer. "The first three months of our marriage we were busy doing... other things, if you'll recall."

Flames ignited in Jana at the sudden recollection Brandon had evoked. It didn't help that he looked and smelled so masculine, either.

"I learned carpentry work when I was a kid," Brandon went on, seemingly oblivious to her tumbling heart. "After you left, I made a workroom in the attic."

"I...I didn't know."

He shrugged. "As you said, there're lots of things we don't know about each other...yet."

"Come on, Mr. Sayer," one of the boys called. "Let's get to work."

A chorus of impatient young voices chimed in.

"I'll be right there," Brandon called. He turned back to Jana. "Guess I'd better get back."

She stole a quick glance back at the refuge again. "I think I'll stay and watch for a while—if you don't mind."

"Sure." Brandon took a minute to stack some blocks beneath the tree and stretch a couple of boards across them, making a little bench. Jana settled herself on it, enjoying the play of Brandon's muscles through his shirt, the close cut of his trousers. He was patient with the boys, explaining how to read the rough blueprint, which tool to use for which job.

How nice it was to sit and watch. Brandon seldom stayed in one spot for long. Always going somewhere, doing something. Though lately, he seemed often to be wherever she was.

Brandon had come to so many of her luncheons that now Jana actually caught herself watching for him. He left flowers on her pillow so often that she was disappointed the few times she'd gone into her room and found none. How easily he'd become a routine part of her day.

Yet she couldn't forget the faces at the windows, watching Brandon along with her. Leona Albright floated into her mind.

Brandon had asked if she'd been involved with anyone during their separation.

Perhaps she should have asked him the same question.

Chapter Fifteen

She simply couldn't look at another wallpaper pattern.

Jana closed the sample book and gave it a push, sending it to the other end of the settee. Much still needed to be done to the bedchambers upstairs. She wanted to decide on a theme for each of the rooms, then select all the fabrics, paint and wallpaper at once, and have everything in place, ready to be installed. The construction crews were still busy working in the parlor and study downstairs, and she'd endured just about all of the commotion she could bear these past weeks. She wanted the workmen to descend on the bedchambers, complete the job quickly and leave.

All she had to do was make the decorating decisions. Jana sighed. Tonight, she didn't want to decide on anything. Her thoughts—and her heart—were elsewhere.

Such as at the women's refuge. Volunteering there

had taken more of her time than she'd anticipated. She'd thought of as but a way to fill her day. Yet now that she'd involved herself there and seen what a worthwhile cause it was, she couldn't back away from it.

As a result, visits to her aunt's suite at the Morgan Hotel had become rushed and brief. Some days she managed only a few minutes there. Aunt Maureen assured her she didn't mind, that it was perfectly all right and everything was under control. But Jana couldn't so easily ignore her responsibilities and commitment.

And at both places, the refuge and the Morgan, Brandon wasn't far from her thoughts.

Over supper tonight, he'd talked with her about what had gone on at his office today. He even ate the meals Jana had insisted Mrs. Boone prepare, and he hadn't complained at all about the work being done on the house. Twice this week he'd come home early to check with the gardeners on the landscaping she'd wanted done in the rear lawn.

It was all a stretch for him, sometimes—she could see that. But he kept at it, kept trying to make her happy.

If only she could believe this was a permanent change, not just the temporary measures he knew were needed to get her to stay.

Jana rose from the settee intending to go up to her room. Brandon had disappeared right after supper and she'd told herself that she should be glad, but instead she'd found herself wondering where he was, what he was doing. The idea of another evening alone in her room held no appeal. Perhaps she could find Brandon, see what he was up to...just this once.

The size of the house would have required a lengthy search to find him, but since only a few of the rooms were liveable her quest would be simpler if she chose to hunt him down. Instead, she asked Charles. Somehow, the butler always knew where everyone and everything was at every conceivable time of the day or night.

Jana climbed the stairs to the second floor, past the bedchambers, down another hallway to a door that stood open. She gazed up the narrow staircase and saw faint light shining at the top. The attic. She'd never been up there, not even during the first three months she'd lived in the house.

Before, she'd thought nothing of it. Now it seemed odd that she hadn't bothered to investigate every inch of her home.

She gathered her skirt and climbed the stairs. The attic occupied about half the space of the house's third floor; the servants' quarters took up the other half, accessed by a different staircase that led directly to the kitchen. The wide-open space contained the usual clutter of boxes and travel trunks; light fixtures dangled from the high ceiling. Tonight, the windows on all three sides of the room stood open, allowing the evening breeze to cool the space.

A space that seemed to shrink before Jana's eyes when she saw Brandon in the far corner.

He still wore his business suit, but his jacket and

necktie were off and his sleeves were rolled back. He stood over a worktable frowning down at something, surrounded by pieces of lumber and all sorts of tools. The sweet scent of sawdust hung in the air.

He appeared so deep in thought that Jana wondered if perhaps she should slip away, leave him to his work. But he looked up suddenly and turned to her.

Jana's heart warmed a little. Could he somehow sense her presence, as she could his?

"I didn't mean to disturb you," she said, lingering near the top of the staircase.

"No, it's fine," he said, waving her over, seemingly genuinely pleased to see her. "Come in."

Jana crossed the room and stood next to him. As always when he was this close, an intimate awareness came to her. How tall he was. His straight shoulders, long legs. Big hands. Strength and muscles. And all of that power exquisitely tempered when he held her hand, assisted her into a carriage, touched her elbow. Gentleness, just for her.

Something changed about Brandon the minute she stopped next to him. Jana sensed it immediately. His shoulders straightened and his chest expanded. A new, different sort of heat wafted from him.

"What are you doing here?" she asked, gesturing to the workbench, pretending not to notice the changes in him, or her reaction to them.

"Designing a trapdoor," Brandon said, nodding toward the diagram on the worktable. "The boys want a trapdoor in the tree house."

"The boys at the refuge?" Jana asked. She smiled. "It's really very good of you to take on this project. You've created quite a stir there, you know."

He frowned. "With the boys?"

"With their mothers."

Brandon rolled his eyes.

"Don't worry," Jana told him. "I'll protect your honor."

He smiled, then shook his head. "Are women always looking for a husband?"

"Usually. It's the goal of every mother to have her daughter marry well," Jana said. "Though not every daughter wants that. Beth's young cousin Audrey seems to be one of the new, modern women."

Brandon shrugged. "That makes her a little out of step with everyone else, doesn't it?"

"Yes, but it seems to suit her," Jana said. "I think Oliver Fisk has a terrible crush on her. I'm not sure how he'll feel when he learns that Audrey believes there's more to life than being a wife."

Brandon gazed down at her. "Is that how you felt?"

The question startled Jana. For a moment, she hesitated. Several months into their separation the answer to that very question had come to her. She wasn't proud of it.

But Brandon deserved to hear it.

"I was in love with the idea of being a bride," Jana said. "I didn't stop to realize that, afterwards, I'd be a wife."

Brandon continued to look at her, and she couldn't tell if her words had hurt him, or confirmed what he already knew.

"My lack of vision created a great hardship on you," Jana said softly. "I'm sorry."

Brandon looked away. "I wasn't much of a husband either. I thought I could go about my life, same as always, and you'd do whatever it was women did all day."

He turned to her once more. "I'm sorry."

"I like you better now," she offered.

"I'm much more likable now," he said, a little grin pulling at his lips.

"And you've become quite a poet," she added, smiling along with him.

Brandon snorted. "Luckily, I'm better at building things than writing poetry. Otherwise, this tree house would collapse, and what would all the mothers think of me then?"

"I think they would all still appreciate what you're doing for the boys. Many of them haven't had a strong male figure in their lives," Jana said.

He pointed to several pieces of wood cut in odd shapes stacked on the end of the workbench. "These are for the younger boys, the ones too little to help with the tree house. All they have to do is nail them together."

"What is it?" Jana asked, tilting her head.

"A birdhouse." Brandon fitted a few of the pieces together, holding them with his fingers. "Walls, floor, roof. See?"

"Oh, yes, of course," Jana said. She shook her head. "I had no idea. Where did you learn to do all of this? From your own father?"

Brandon let the wood fall to the table. He turned away and began sorting through a small bin of nails. "Are you going to the refuge tomorrow?"

"Did I say the wrong thing, asking about your father?"

He kept digging in the bin, his back to her.

"Brandon?" Jana touched his arm. She knew his father—and his mother—were dead; Aunt Maureen had learned that from the private detective she'd hired to investigate Brandon's past shortly after he'd asked to court Jana.

Yet Jana hadn't known the mention of either of them would be so painful for Brandon. She mentally berated herself for her thoughtlessness. And for not knowing this about her husband. After all the time they'd courted and been married, living under the same roof, sharing a bed, and she had no idea.

She'd been a terrible wife. And still was.

"I'm sorry," Jana said softly, apologizing to him for the second time this evening. "I didn't realize the memory was so painful. I wouldn't have brought it up, if I'd known. I'm truly sorry, Brandon."

Another moment passed and finally he looked back at her. His expression was like nothing she'd ever witnessed. Angry? Hurt? Annoyed? She wasn't sure.

Brandon drew in a breath, as if pulling up his courage—or, perhaps, forcing down his emotions.

"My father died when I was a child," he said softly. Then he cleared his voice and pushed on, forcing a little more strength into his voice. "I never knew the man.

My mother and I lived in Europe until I was about ten years old."

When his mother died, Jana knew from the private detective's report that Brandon had been raised by his grandfather, Winston Delaney, owner of New York's largest shipyard, several shipping lines, and most everything else in that state.

Jana gazed up at Brandon, saw the pain in his expression that the memory had brought on. She pressed her palm to his cheek and he turned into her caress, closing his eyes for a few seconds.

Yet that wasn't enough. Jana rose on her toes to loop her arms around his neck, wanting nothing more than to comfort him, ease his suffering, make things better for him.

Brandon held back, then circled her waist and drew her near, burying his face against her neck. They clung together for a long time, then Brandon lifted his head. As they gazed into each other's eyes, another long moment passed. Then he kissed her.

Softly, he touched his lips to hers, blending their mouths together. Jana gasped at the delight of it. Brandon moaned low in his throat. He deepened the kiss, and she let him, parting her lips and welcoming the familiarity that their time apart hadn't erased.

He pulled her closer, full against him. Jana dug her fingers into his hair. Their kiss grew hotter. His thigh snuggled against her intimately and she felt the hard length of him through her skirt. His palm cupped her breast. She gasped. He groaned and leaned her back over the workbench. Jana looped her leg around his, keeping him close.

He lifted his head, passion burning in his eyes. "You...you told me you didn't want us to..."

"I don't," she said, then pulled his head down again.

He gave her a searing kiss, then raised up once more. "Then we should...stop."

His hot breath puffed against her mouth. Her heart raced. "Yes...yes, let's stop."

"All right." Brandon devoured her lips once more. She let him. Jana kissed him back, welcoming his touch, his warmth, the intimacy she'd done without for so long.

Brandon pulled his lips from hers and gazed into her eyes. She slid her palm to his chest and felt his heart pounding. Then he eased away, standing upright, drawing her up with him, off of the workbench.

Yet he didn't release her completely. He held her in his arms, but not so close that they touched. Full contact between them would bring on an outpouring of emotion that would end only one way. Jana knew it. The look on Brandon's face told her that he knew the same.

He backed away, letting the cool breeze swirl between them. Jana straightened her blouse and smoothed her skirt. Without another word, they left the attic. Brandon stopped at the door to his bedchamber and she walked on to hers. With her hand on the knob, she looked back down the hallway at him.

Go to him? If she did, Jana knew she could never

leave his side—let alone this house. She turned away and went into her room, closing the door soundly behind her.

Brandon stared at the empty space she'd just occupied, the thud of the closing door still ringing in his ears. He grumbled under his breath and pushed into his own room.

Fine thing. Acting the gentleman, dropping by luncheons, eating at places like that ridiculous Peacock Tea Room, writing poetry, sending flowers—and here he was still hard and achy and going to bed alone.

Brandon stalked across the room, dropped his suspenders and yanked off his shirt. He stopped at the window and pulled his undershirt over his head, then sent it flying across the room.

Fine thing. Hard and achy and going to bed alone while his wife—*his wife*—slept only yards away.

Cool air drifted through the open window causing his hot skin to tingle. He braced his arm against the casing and gazed into the moonlit yard.

He'd done everything he knew to court Jana. Wracked his brain for poems, left flowers, brought gifts, eaten strange meals, let her turn the house upside down, asked about her plans for the day, told her about his. Yet none of it seemed to help their situation.

And, certainly, none of it had gotten him into her bed. He was nearly at his wits' end. He didn't know what else he could do to make her happy.

Oh, she was pleasant enough. Friendly, kind, but still distant.

The memory of their first three months of marriage sprang into Brandon's mind. The ache deepened at the recollection.

He and Jana had made love so easily. They fit together perfectly, mind and body. As a new bride, she hadn't minded his gentle direction, his suggestions. She'd whispered to him things that she enjoyed, things she wanted to do.

Yet their lovemaking hadn't ended there. They cuddled all night. In the mornings when Brandon had to leave for work, he couldn't get out of the bed for her reaching out to him. Not always to make love again, but just to touch him. To rub his back. To feel his chest. She let him caress her.

More often than not, Jana asked him to stay. Not to go to work that day but to crawl back in bed with her. He always gave her a tender kiss and left anyway.

He'd thought his business holdings were so important back then. What difference would it have made to those deals if he'd done as she asked? Probably very little.

Yet how much difference would it have made to his marriage if he'd stayed home with Jana those mornings? He might be the one expecting an heir now, just as Noah Carmichael was.

What a damn fool he'd been.

Brandon cursed under his breath at the lunacy of his decisions back then. What the hell had he been thinking?

And what a terrible husband he'd been.

Turning away from the window, Brandon went into

the adjoining bathroom and flipped on the light. A harsh glare lit the white ceramic tile. He stood over the washbasin for a while, then turned on the tap and splashed cold water on his face.

He straightened and dragged a towel down his face, looking at himself in the mirror. Why hadn't he paid better attention to Jana back then—other than in the bedroom? Why hadn't he seen that she missed her aunt and friends in San Francisco, that the decorator and cook—and maybe all the servants—disregarded her every want? If he'd been a better husband, she wouldn't have left.

And he sure as hell wouldn't be in here all by himself right now.

Brandon tossed the towel away and drew in a breath.

What next? What else? What could he do now that would bring Jana back to him, keep her from leaving again? Maybe if he tried to—

He stopped as a new idea sprang into his head. Why not do the one thing he and Jana had both liked so much early in their marriage?

Why not simply get her into bed?

Upstairs in the attic this evening they might have made love right then and there if Brandon hadn't been so concerned about Jana's wishes. If he'd gone ahead and made love to her—something they both seemed to want—things might at this very minute be settled between them.

Of course. It made perfect sense. Brandon nodded his head in the silent room.

He'd just get her into bed. That would solve everything.

Chapter Sixteen

Certainly nothing was wrong with wanting one's own husband. Was there?

Jana caught herself contemplating the question as she sat behind the desk in the office of the women's refuge. Contemplating, too, what might have happened if Brandon hadn't come to his senses in the attic last night.

Warmth swelled in Jana as she recalled the details of their encounter. His arms around her. His lips on hers. The feel of his body pressed against hers. A rush of memories came back to her.

She hadn't had the strength or the willpower to tell him to stop last night. Making love would be the worst thing that could happen between them. She knew that. But still…

Jana pushed herself up from the chair and drew in a breath. An apology was in order. She'd go outside right now and tell Brandon how sorry she was about what had happened—almost—between them. He'd done the right thing and respected her wishes. And she...

Wanted him.

Jana jerked to a stop in the doorway as the realization formed in the pit of her stomach. She pressed her lips together, fighting off the idea, then unable to, let it come fully into her mind.

Yes, she wanted Brandon. Her husband. She let the notion play in her mind, the very thought sending a warm chill over her. For a long moment she luxuriated in the feeling, allowed herself to ignore the folly of that possibility. And how delightful it was.

Then, just as she had in London, Jana pushed the nonsense away. She steeled her emotions and continued on, determined to do what she *had* to do...just as she had in London.

But at that moment, Oliver Fisk walked through the front door, satchel in hand.

"Another class today?" Jana asked, thinking that she hadn't seen his name on this afternoon's schedule.

"Well, no...not exactly." Oliver leaned around her, gazing down the hallway. "I, ah, I couldn't quite remember when I was supposed to teach again, so I thought I'd drop by."

"I see."

"Strictly business," Oliver said, looking at her now. "That's all. Business."

Jana raised an eyebrow at him. "I don't suppose your

forgetfulness over the schedule has anything to do with Audrey, does it?"

Oliver's cheeks flushed and he blinked rapidly at her from behind his lenses. "Oh, no. Of course not. Why, I never even thought for a moment that—"

"It's all right if you're attracted to her," Jana said, giving him an understanding smile.

A deeper shade of pink came to Oliver's cheeks, then he looked away, shaking his head. "Silly of me, really," he said quietly. "Thinking a beautiful, intelligent girl like Audrey would give me a second look."

"Don't be so hard on yourself," Jana insisted. "You have a great deal to offer any woman."

Oliver lifted a shoulder. "I do have a bit of money— a good bit, actually. A trust fund from my grandfather which will be under my control in a few more years."

"And you're quite intelligent yourself," Jana pointed out. "A man with a responsible position."

"For as long as it lasts," Oliver said. He shook his head. "Audrey deserves so much more than someone like me."

"Audrey is a bit unconventional. A modern woman with modern ideas." Jana touched his arm. "Don't give up yet."

Oliver shrugged, then gestured down the hallway. "Since I'm here, I'll visit with the ladies for a few minutes. See what they thought of my class."

"That's a good idea," Jana agreed.

Her heart ached a little watching Oliver head down

the hallway. He saw the futility of his desire. No matter how much he wanted things to be different, it seemed it was not to be.

His plight gave her strength. Jana squared her shoulders. She, too, had to do what must be done. With her marriage, and her husband.

No matter how much it hurt.

Yet her good intentions faltered once more as she walked into the rear yard and her gaze homed in on Brandon. Up in a tree, he balanced on one of the limbs as he oversaw the boys working on the tree house. He pointed and Jana heard the deep rumbling of his voice. The boys nodded and worked diligently.

This was hardly the time to bother him, Jana decided. And hardly the place to discuss her wanton behavior last night.

But before she could return to the refuge, Brandon spotted her. He called her name, then ignored the steps nailed to the side of the tree, grabbed a low branch and swung to the ground.

He wore his work clothes. Jana's heart fluttered at the sight of him, still.

"How's it going?" she asked as he walked over.

He glanced back at the tree house. "Almost finished, trapdoor and all."

"You've got yourself quite a crew," Jana said, nodding toward the smaller boys gathered around a makeshift workbench. "Are those the birdhouses you showed me last night in the attic?"

Jana gasped, mentally berating herself for mentioning the attic, calling to bear the things they'd done there. Goodness, what would he think of her?

Brandon frowned. "Were you in the attic with me last night?"

"Why, yes, of course I was," Jana said, suddenly a little miffed that he couldn't remember. She'd chided herself over and over about what had happened, and all the while it meant nothing to Brandon?

"I came up into the attic to see your workshop," Jana told him. "You were at your workbench and you showed me the birdhouses you'd cut out."

"You did?" Brandon scratched his head. "Then what happened?"

"You explained what they were, and then I thoughtlessly mentioned your family—which I apologized for—and then we kissed." Jana pressed her lips together. "I can't believe you really don't remember this."

"Oh, yes," Brandon said, nodding. He frowned again. "Was that you I kissed?"

"Of course it was," she insisted. "We kissed and then you touched my—"

Jana stopped, seeing the tiniest quirk on his lips. He was teasing her.

"Your breast," Brandon said, his voice low and mellow. "I touched your breast. The left one. My favorite."

Jana's stomach heated, sending a plume of warmth up her neck and across her cheeks. He glanced down at her breasts and they tingled at his gaze.

"I knew you remembered," she said, trying to muster some annoyance with him, but failing miserably.

Brandon leaned in a little. "I told you, Jana, I remember *everything*."

And suddenly *everything* sprang up between them, unseen but with a force that seemed to capture the two of them, bind them together now just as their lovemaking had done all those months ago.

A voice intruded, breaking the spell between then. Jana realized someone was calling her name. She turned and saw one of the young girls heading toward her.

"Mrs. Sayer? There's a woman here to see you," she reported, then dashed away to where the other girls played across the yard.

"I'd better go," Jana said, lifting her gaze to meet Brandon's.

He gave her a little grin, a secretive, knowing grin.

"You'd better get back to work too," Jana said, catching sight of the younger boys from the corner of her eye. A disagreement had developed, apparently, over whose turn it was to use the hammer.

Brandon seemed to take it in stride as he gave her a final grin and walked away.

Jana watched for a moment as he stood towering over the boys, listening while they all tried to talk at once. Yet for all his greater height, strength and authority, none of the children seemed frightened of him. He knelt and spoke to them, and in a matter of moments, heads bobbed in agreement and the work started up again.

Her heart warmed at the sight. She had no idea Brandon could be so good with children. The notion twisted tightly inside her.

"Mrs. Sayer?"

Jana turned when she heard her name again, but it wasn't one of the young girls calling her this time. Jana's heart seemed to skip a beat.

Leona Albright stood in front of her.

Instinctively, Jana cast a glance at Brandon. He seemed to hear Leona's voice also—or had he instinctively sensed her arrival?—and turned to face the two of them. An awkward moment passed before Leona spoke.

"I heard the call had gone out for volunteers," Leona said, "so I decided to stop by and have a look for myself."

"That's very kind of you," Jana said, drawing on her years of etiquette training to see her though, when all the while her mind was reeling.

Leona scanned the play yard, nodding slowly. "Everything I see here seems to be in perfect order," she declared.

Her gaze fell on Brandon as he walked over to join them, and Jana was overwhelmed with the urge to throw herself in front of her husband, a wild, irrational notion that she couldn't shake.

"Leona," Brandon greeted, standing close to Jana's side. "Don't tell me you're thinking of volunteering."

"Oh, no, of course not. But I thought I might throw my support behind the effort." Leona turned to Jana. "If it's wanted, of course."

The woman had done nothing untoward. She'd said nothing inappropriate. Her errand here today was, obviously, a desire to truly help the refuge. Yet there was something about the way she looked at Brandon. Not desirous, the way Jana knew she herself had looked at him only minutes ago. But it was something. Something that Jana couldn't name. Something that left her disquieted.

"The refuge would greatly appreciate anything you might do to help," Jana told her, pleased that she'd managed to sound gracious.

"Then, with your permission, I'd like to—"

Leona stopped and turned her attention to Oliver Fisk as he approached. Her gaze dipped, ran the length of him, and a slow smile spread over her face.

"Brandon, do introduce us," she said, shifting her shoulders and arching her back ever so slightly.

Brandon did as she asked, and when introduced, Oliver seemed to shrink back from her, much as a lamb would from an approaching wolf.

"So you're the editor of the *Messenger*," Leona said, slipping closer to him. "I think you and I have something in common."

Oliver gulped. "What—what would that be?"

"I'll give you a detailed explanation." Leona slid her arm through Oliver's, drawing him closer until her breast rested against his arm. "I'm very good at…details."

"Oh—well—yes, but—" Oliver's eyes widened as Leona guided him across the yard and into the refuge.

A bit befuddled, Jana watched them disappear, then turned to Brandon.

"What do you think she meant by that?" she asked.

A grin bloomed on his lips and he tried to contain it but couldn't.

Jana gasped. "Do you think Leona Albright has designs on—Oliver?"

"So it seems," Brandon said, twisting his lips. He nodded toward the boys. "I'd better get back there, see what's going on. Will you be ready to go home soon?"

It sounded so simple when he said it. The two of them. Traveling around the city in his carriage, as any husband and wife would do. Going home.

"I only have a few more things to do," Jana said.

Brandon nodded and headed to the rear of the yard where the boys worked. She went back inside and finished up the list of potential volunteers she intended to contact, then pinned on her hat and gathered her wrap and handbag when Brandon came into the office.

In the carriage, Brandon sat in the seat across from her, as he always did. Usually he looked out the window, giving her only an occasional glance, but today he seemed fascinated by the very sight of her. Or at least her bosom. That seemed to be where his gaze veered, every time she cast a glance his way. Her breasts. The left one. His favorite.

Relieved when they finally arrived home, Jana told Charles in the vestibule that she wanted supper in her room, then went upstairs and undressed. The day had been warm and she was glad to be rid of her corset, bustle and petticoats. Abbie came to her room and helped her change into a day dress, a comfortable, lightweight garment.

When a knock sounded at the door, Abbie answered it, then turned to Jana.

"It's Charles," she reported. "He says that Mr. Sayer wants you to come downstairs immediately."

"Has someone arrived?" Jana asked, though she couldn't imagine anyone dropping by at this hour.

"No, ma'am," Abbie said. "Mr. Sayer says he wants you. Now."

Chapter Seventeen

Brandon on the rear lawn? Jana made her way through the house, as Charles had directed her, wondering what sort of problem would cause Brandon to send for her, and insist that she join him immediately. He'd never done that before.

And that was the sole reason Jana went downstairs in her state of dress. The lavender day dress with nothing underneath but pantalettes and a chemise was certainly not appropriate attire for anyplace in the house or on the grounds, except her bedchamber.

Stepping out onto the porch, Jana gazed across the rear yard. Stone paths wound through the shrubs and flowers, the fountains and the palm trees. She didn't see Brandon but knew where he most likely was.

Jana's slippers brushed the soft grass as she crossed to the area of the yard the gardeners had been working on recently. She'd asked them to construct an arched arbor in a tall hedgerow, a portal to a portion of the yard that she decided would make a lovely private garden. An isolated spot, obscured from the house by the hedges, it offered solitude from problems, troubles and unpopular houseguests. A perfect respite after a busy day.

She stepped through the arbor and spotted Brandon standing in the center of the garden, still dressed in his work clothes, taking in the area with a critical eye.

"Brandon?"

He turned quickly. "You're here. Good. I wanted you to see—"

His words stopped abruptly when his gaze fell on her. He shifted, and drew in a quick breath. Jana flushed from head to toe. She wasn't sure which of them was more conscious of her diminished dress—Brandon or herself.

For an instant, Jana thought she should leave. But somehow, she couldn't bring herself to move from the spot. Brandon wanted her. It couldn't be more obvious. And that was an allure too potent to ignore.

He walked toward her, his gaze still wandering. "I, ah, I wanted you to come out here and…and…" Brandon stopped in front of her and rubbed his forehead. He glanced down at the ground, then at her face again. "Damn if I can remember."

Jana flushed anew with the power her mere presence held. Brandon Sayer, revered by so many for his brilliant mind, rendered momentarily brainless because she appeared before him without her corset, bustle and petticoats.

"The garden," she said, smiling gently. "You probably wanted me to see the garden."

"Oh, yes. Of course." Brandon gave himself a little shake and gestured with his hand. "I stopped by before I went to the refuge this afternoon and saw that the gardeners were finished. I wanted you to see it this evening. To make sure this is what you wanted."

Jana deliberately turned her attention to the improvements she'd asked the gardeners to make, conscious all the while of Brandon's hot gaze still climbing over her. Conscious, too, of the warmth that grew inside of her. She forced her mind to the task at hand, taking in the flower bed, the shrubs, the statues and benches she'd asked for. It all looked especially cozy in the fading evening sun.

"It's lovely," she said.

"You're sure?" he asked.

No, not really. But she seemed to be having as much trouble concentrating as Brandon.

Why had he never worn work clothes during the first three months of their marriage? His ruggedness appealed to her in an entirely different way. And had he looked at her the way he did now? With raw desire in his expression? Desire that spilled onto her?

Or was it just their months of separation that intensified everything?

"Would you take a look around?" Brandon asked, gesturing around the garden. "Just to make sure the gardeners did everything you wanted?"

"All right," she agreed, though the thought sprang into her mind that leaving might be more prudent.

Brandon walked alongside her as they made their way slowly through the garden. He asked about every statue, every flower bed, every plant, making sure it fit her specifications.

When she'd initially assigned him the task of overseeing the gardeners' work, it had been more to annoy him than because she really wanted a private garden. His ranting about duties and responsibilities had provoked her and she'd wanted to give him a taste of his own medicine. But the garden had turned out quite nicely.

"I know you wanted this bench to face the other way," Brandon said as they stood in front of it, "but then the morning sun would have been in your face, so I had it changed."

"It's perfect." Jana gazed up at him as evening shadows cast them both in dim light. "In fact, everything is perfect. You did an excellent job overseeing the gardeners. Thank you."

He nodded and allowed himself a small smile, satisfied with himself and the work.

"Good," Brandon said. "I want you to be happy... with everything. And, in fact, I thought it would be nice if you and I— Here we are."

Jana turned in the direction that had taken Brandon's attention and saw three of the house servants coming through the arbor, carrying a quilt and two wicker hampers.

"What's this?" Jana asked.

"Late supper," Brandon said. He spoke to the servants, directing them to set up the picnic, then said, "I thought it would be nice if you and I ate out here, just so you can get the feel of the garden."

Jana glanced at the arbor and considered making a dash for it. This late supper of Brandon's had romantic interlude written all over it. After last night in the attic, she wasn't sure she was strong enough to stand up to her own edict of allowing no intimacy between them.

But he was trying awfully hard to see that she was happy. She couldn't doubt that. He'd overseen the garden, made sure it met her specifications, and he'd arranged with the servants to bring their supper here.

Fourteen months ago he'd not wanted her at his breakfast table. He barely spoke during supper. And now he'd brought her a picnic in the garden.

"Is it all right?" Brandon asked, sounding genuinely concerned that he might have done the wrong thing.

Jana drew in a determined breath. What better opportunity would she have to prove to herself that she could resist Brandon? That she could sit under the stars in this isolated garden and not succumb to his charms?

That she could walk away from him when their thirty days together were up and know she'd done the right thing.

"It's a wonderful idea," Jana said.

The servants fussed over the meal for a few minutes, then hurried away. Brandon offered his hand and Jana lowered herself onto the pale blue quilt, drawing her legs under her and pulling down her skirt. Brandon plopped down beside her, close, but not too close.

"Let's see, what have we got?" he murmured, as he lifted a bottle of wine from one of the open hampers. "This looks good."

Everything, indeed, looked good. The servants had spread out platters of grapes and strawberries, cheese and ham and chunks of bread to go along with the wine. Jana placed a little of everything on two china plates while Brandon poured the wine.

"Shall we drink to something?" he asked.

"Such as what?" she asked, accepting a crystal glass.

"Hum…let's see. Our past wasn't all that pleasant, and our future is a little cloudy," Brandon said. "I guess that just leaves us with the present."

"To the present," Jana said, clinking her glass against his. She sipped the wine and smiled. "This 'present' is very nice."

"The only way it could be better is if you let me touch your breasts."

"What?"

He sipped his wine and let his gaze fall on her bosom. "You have the most beautiful breasts I've ever seen, or touched, or…or, well, you remember the things we used to do."

Heat rushed through Jana at the recollection. Her memory didn't fail her.

"I owe you an apology for last night in the attic," Jana

said, setting her wineglass aside. "You've done as I asked, respected my wish that we…that you…"

"That I remain celibate in my own home with my own wife in bed in the next room?"

He hadn't said it with rancor, yet it bothered Jana just the same.

"Anyway," she continued, "I owe you an apology. It was my fault. It started when I touched your cheek—"

"No, Jana. All you have to do is walk into the room." He grinned. "Or into a garden."

"I should leave."

"Don't bother. It won't matter." He touched her arm, stilling her. "I want you every minute of every day and every night."

"Why are you telling me this?"

"I learned fourteen months ago not to take anything for granted. A very hard, very painful lesson, but I learned it." Brandon was silent for a while. "I never told you why I wrote you in London, asked you to come home."

He hadn't, she realized. Even in the letter, he hadn't explained his demand for her return. Simply said that she was to come home.

"No, you never told me," she said.

Brandon studied the horizon for a moment, then spoke.

"A few months ago, Charles asked for a day off. He said the other servants requested it also. Oddly enough, Mr. Perkins at the office had asked the same thing." Brandon turned to Jana. "It was the day before Christmas Eve, and I hadn't realized it."

"Oh, Brandon…"

"I got a good hard look at my future, and I didn't like what I saw." He drew in a breath. "So, I wrote to you."

"And when I got here, I asked for a divorce," Jana said, feeling a little ashamed after hearing how he'd spent Christmas.

"That did surprise me," Brandon admitted. He looked into her eyes. "I love you, Jana."

She looked away. "Don't say that. You know we decided to wait until the four weeks were up and then decide what to do."

"I love you." Brandon shrugged. "That won't change—whether you stay or go."

They gazed at each other for a minute and Jana saw nothing but sincerity in his eyes. She pressed her lips together, forbidding herself to say anything.

Brandon seemed not to notice her dilemma as he took up the plate of food and ate. She did the same, picking at the fruit, the cheese. Then, with a deep sigh, Brandon lay back and stretched out on the quilt, tucking his hands behind his head.

"Tired?" she asked.

"Those boys at the refuge work me harder than anything at the office." He grinned. "Can't remember the last time I climbed a tree."

Jana smiled. She couldn't remember the last time she had *enjoyed* watching anyone climb a tree.

"Look." Brandon pointed toward the sky. "The first star of the evening."

Jana turned toward the horizon and saw a star shining in the closing darkness.

"Make a wish," he said.

She closed her eyes for a few seconds, made her wish, then turned to Brandon.

"I know what you wished for," she said. "Success with your Jennings project."

He raised a brow at her. "Is that what you think?"

"I know it's important to you."

"I wouldn't waste a wish on that project," Brandon said. "Not to sound immodest, but the Jennings building needs no magic. I've already seen to everything. The renovations are underway and new tenants are lining up, eagerly filling my pockets with their lease money."

"Isn't that a bit premature?" she asked. Though they'd had this conversation before, the knowledge that he'd gone ahead with the project bothered Jana. "What if the *Messenger* somehow pulls through? What will people think of you if that happens?"

"They'll think I'm a complete idiot and my reputation will be ruined." He gave her a quick, confident smile. "But that won't happen."

"You hope," Jana said. But she'd noticed that Brandon had stopped reading the *Messenger*. A sure indication that he'd made up his mind, once and for all.

"It won't happen, Jana." Brandon closed this topic of conversation by shifting on the ground and gesturing toward the sky again. "I know what you wished for."

"I'll bet you don't."

"You wished that you could see me naked."

"Brandon!"

"Don't bother to lie," he told her. "I see that look on your face."

She swatted him on the arm. "You're certainly full of yourself tonight."

Brandon chuckled. "All right, then. Choose another star and make another wish. I'll still know what you wished for."

Jana watched him for a minute and he gave her a look that challenged her to do just that. She couldn't resist.

She lay back on the quilt beside him, but not so close that they touched. "Let's see. I'll need to find the perfect star for this wish."

Darkness had fallen, bringing out the moon and thousands of stars. Her gaze combed the sky for a moment, then she squeezed her eyes closed and cast her wish into the heavens.

"There," she said. "It's done. What did I wish for?"

Brandon made a show of touching his forehead with his fingertips and furrowing his brow as if receiving some divine knowledge.

"Your wish," he announced, "is for me to touch your breasts."

"It is not!"

In the blink of an eye, he rolled toward her and pushed himself up on his elbow, their bodies touching, his face inches from hers.

"Are you sure?" he asked softly.

Breath left Jana in a little wheeze at the memories this position evoked. How many times had they lain together this way? Him above her? His warm breath on her cheek? His hand trailing down her jaw, to her throat, to her—

"Well?" he asked, his voice low and mellow. "I remember that you used to like it when I…"

Instead of describing anything more, Brandon touched his finger to that particular spot behind her ear, the one that caused her to shiver, as it did now. Slowly, he dragged his fingertip down her throat, to her chest until it skimmed her breast where it swelled from her dress. He lowered his head, panting hot breath on the spot.

"You let me touch you last night. Here," he murmured and brushed his knuckles across the underside of her breast.

Jana gasped.

"Beautiful…" He moved his hand to her other breast, brushing it with his fingertips. Then he cupped it with his palm and squeezed it gently. He kneaded it, sliding his hand upward.

Jana held her breath, the exquisite feel, the anticipation keeping her speechless.

Higher his hand rose, approaching the crest. Jana pushed her breasts outward, filling his hand. He inched closer, closer, then pulled his hand away.

"Sorry," Brandon said, drawing away from her and sitting up.

Jana lay there for a moment, the unfulfilled moment holding her in its grip. Then she too sat up.

"Sorry," Brandon said again, glancing sideways at her. "When I get near you I just..."

He didn't say anything else, but he didn't have to. Jana knew what he meant. She felt it herself.

Brandon pushed himself to his feet. "Let's go inside."

She just gazed up at him in the darkness.

"Don't misunderstand," he said. "Say the word and we'll make love right now, right here under the stars. Or upstairs in bed. Or both."

"Both?"

He looked slightly pained. "It's been a long time."

Jana accepted his outstretched hand and got to her feet. They walked into the house together. At the foot of the staircase, Brandon stopped.

"You go on up," he said. "I'll stay down here for a while."

She wondered if he didn't trust himself to remain outside her bedchamber door tonight, after what had just happened.

She wondered if she trusted herself to leave him out there.

"Good night," Brandon said, then turned and disappeared through the dimly lit house.

Jana stood on the bottom step, watching him go, her heart tumbling in her chest.

God help her, she was falling in love with her husband. Falling in love with Brandon, all over again.

But she couldn't. That could never happen. A life together for the two of them was impossible.

She had to leave this place—quickly. She never should have agreed to this arrangement, this trial period together to work on their marriage.

Jana turned and raced up the steps, her heart pounding, tears pushing against her eyes.

She couldn't stay. Because no matter how hard she tried, no matter what words she chose, or how reasonable she attempted to make it sound, she could never explain to Brandon how she'd kept his baby a secret from him all these months.

Chapter Eighteen

"This—this is *scandalous*."

Jana struggled to remain expressionless as she sat across the desk from Oliver Fisk. No easy task, given that his eyes bulged and his cheeks had reddened—not to mention the fact that he was right.

"Unconventional," she admitted. "But—"

"*Mrs. Sayer.*" He glanced over his shoulder, as if to assure himself once more that the door to the office of the women's refuge was still firmly closed, then turned to Jana once again. "This whole thing is…well, it's positively shocking! Appalling! Outrageous—"

"And it just might save your newspaper."

"No…"

Jana picked up the stack of papers Oliver had moments ago read over, then dropped as if they'd suddenly burst into flames beneath his fingers. She'd been up half the night writing them.

After what had happened in the attic, and what had gone on in the garden, Jana knew without a doubt that her feelings for Brandon had turned into love. She'd very nearly given herself to him—twice in two days.

But she couldn't allow that to happen. So she'd walked the floor nearly all night trying to think, trying to decide what to do. And this is what she'd come up with. After hours of work, then coming to the refuge today and lying in wait for Oliver Fisk to appear for his tutoring session with the women, Jana was determined to make her idea work.

Oliver was less than enthusiastic.

"It's a good idea," she insisted, pushing the papers toward him.

"A good idea?" he repeated, his eyes growing even wider. "You want me to run a column in the *Messenger*, a column dealing with women's issues?"

"Yes."

"And *you* intend to write it?"

"Yes, Oliver, that's exactly right. You've just read samples of the types of articles I want to write. Topics such as proper etiquette, table settings, writing invitations and thank-you notes. Problems with child-rearing, advice on handling money, how to deal with an uncooperative landlord," Jana explained. "You've seen the women here at the refuge, Oliver, you know they're interested in that sort of thing, that they need the information to better themselves. So do women all over the city."

"Well, yes, but—"

"It would be a public service," Jana told him. "Really."

Oliver reluctantly took the papers from her hand and shuffled through them.

"But *this*?" he exclaimed. "An advice column titled Ask Mrs. Avery? Questions about how to handle nosy neighbors and problem in-laws, husbands suspected of cheating? It's scandalous."

"It will sell newspapers," Jana insisted. "Look, Oliver, I know how desperately you want to keep the *Messenger* going. I know how hard you've tried, how hard you've worked. But the truth is, circulation is continuing to spiral downward. You can't compete with the *Times*. Brandon is going to close the newspaper."

Oliver shifted in his chair, his expression admitting that she was right even if he wouldn't say the words aloud.

"Your only hope, as I see it, is to do something drastic. Something dynamic. Something to draw in a whole new audience." Jana tapped her finger against the stack of papers. "Something such as this."

"Need I remind you," Oliver pointed out, drawing himself up a little, "that the only time it's fit for a lady to have her name in print is for her wedding announcement and her charitable work."

"That's why we're going to keep my involvement a secret," Jana said. "I'll write the articles under an assumed name, and the advice column under the name Mrs. Avery, and pass them discreetly to you here at the refuge. No one will know I'm behind them."

"I can't let you do this," Oliver insisted, shaking his head.

"Can *you* write articles on etiquette?" she challenged.

"Of course I could," he insisted, then lifted the papers and admitted, "But I couldn't do them as well as you have here. Obviously, you're coming at the subject from the right perspective—a woman's point of view. I can't duplicate that."

"Then why not let me do this?"

"Because if anyone finds out you're behind this, and that I've allowed you to compromise yourself," Oliver said, his voice rising to near panic, "your husband will *kill me.*"

Jana sat back. She couldn't argue with that. Brandon would be furious if he found out she was involved in this scheme. It was, truly, a scandal.

Yet that hadn't been Jana's concern when she'd come up with the idea last night.

"And my being a party to this thing? Subjecting his wife to a scandal of this magnitude?" Oliver shook his head again. "Mr. Sayer would kill me. I know he would."

"Then we'll have to make sure he never finds out," Jana said. Yet she knew she would tell Brandon herself when the time was right, when it suited her, and she would make sure, of course, that Brandon held no ill will toward Oliver.

Jana let a few minutes pass before she spoke again. "It's a good idea. You know it is."

He nodded glumly and ruffled through the corners of the papers. "It's a perfect idea. I wish I'd thought of it myself. Appeal to a whole new market. An emerging market. If men won't read the *Messenger* then aim it at women. It's brilliant, really. And…and it just might save the newspaper."

"Then we have to try it," Jana said.

Oliver stared down at the papers for a long while, then looked up at her. He drew in a deep breath, then let it out slowly. "Yes, we do."

Jana heaved a sigh of relief. "Good. You can run these articles tomorrow. I'll write more tonight and you can pick them up here at the refuge when you come to tutor."

"What about the questions?" he asked, holding up the Ask Mrs. Avery advice column.

"If women actually write in with questions, I'll answer them," Jana said. "In the meantime, I'll make them up, just as I did for this column."

"Which brings up the whole issue of journalistic integrity, not to mention professional ethics," Oliver mused, rising from his chair. "But what difference will that make, after your husband has pounded me to a pulp?"

"That won't happen," Jana said, though even to her own ears, her words didn't sound all that reassuring.

Oliver shoved the papers into his satchel and left the office mumbling under his breath.

Jana sat back in the chair, telling herself she should be pleased with herself. She'd gotten Oliver to go along with her plan to save the newspaper. The *Messenger* was doomed. Oliver knew it. This idea of hers to write for the women of the city just might be the key to keeping the presses running.

But deep in her heart, Jana knew the truth. She'd used Oliver. Used him to ruin Brandon's Jennings project.

Used him to force Brandon to let her leave.

She'd tried everything else. Tearing the house apart, driving Brandon out of his study, changing the meals. Twice she'd asked him outright to let her leave and he had refused. Everything she did was ineffective.

And on top of all that, Brandon was now being warm and caring. The perfect husband. Last night under the stars he even told her he loved her.

Jana rose from the chair and walked to the window. It offered little in the way of a view, just the side of the building next door and a glimpse of the street out front.

She curled her hand into a fist and bounced it against the windowsill. Desperate measures were called for. If the *Messenger* pulled out of its slump and began to flourish, Brandon would be forced to keep it in operation. Doing so would necessitate canceling his Jennings project. When she revealed to him that she'd been behind the whole thing, he would send her packing.

All the effort he'd put into the project would be for naught. Money spent, never to be recovered. His business reputation tarnished. Brandon would be furious with her. Business, above all else, was what mattered to him. Jana had learned that the very first night in his house as his new bride. She'd seen nothing since that changed her mind.

She was certain he would recover from both the economic and personal hardship of the ruined project, in time. But he would never forgive her.

Yes, desperate action was called for. Jana gazed out the window at the passing traffic. She knew about desperation.

A miserable bride, a fearful escape from a cold husband, and a surprise pregnancy. That's how she'd found herself fourteen months ago. She had thought she was simply seasick from the crossing. But after a week on dry land in London brought no improvement, Jana confided in Aunt Maureen.

Yet when she learned that, indeed, a baby was on the way, Jana had been elated. Her first reaction had been nothing but pure joy. She couldn't have been happier.

Aunt Maureen wanted to return to America right away, confront Brandon, put the marriage back on track. But Jana wouldn't hear of it. A transatlantic and transcontinental journey were trying enough under ideal circumstances. She wouldn't jeopardize her unborn baby with the attempt. She stayed in London, made her aunt promise to keep her secret, and had her baby there.

A wave of longing rose in Jana, sure and strong, and troubling.

Why should she have to choose between her baby and her husband? Why couldn't she have both?

She walked the floor of their London town house

many nights contemplating that very question. But she knew the answer.

Marriage to Brandon had been an absolute nightmare during the first three months they were together. He'd been withdrawn and distant, uncaring and cold much of the time. He'd been so dreadful, she herself couldn't live with him.

What chance would an innocent baby have?

When she'd taken her first look at her child, after all those hours of labor, and held the tiny, defenseless thing in her arms, Jana knew right then she would never subject the baby to Brandon. At that moment, she'd fallen in love with her child. It was as if her own heart had somehow attached itself to the newly beating one. She'd protect this baby with her life. She'd kill for this baby. All she cared about was what was best for her child. Nothing else mattered. Certainly not Brandon.

A divorce was the only option. Jana made that decision shortly after giving birth. She'd get a divorce and not tell Brandon about the baby. If he knew, he'd refuse to grant her the divorce and insist that she and the child remain with him. Jana simply wouldn't hear of it. The baby deserved so much more from a father, from a home. It was her duty, her responsibility to ensure a safe, happy future for her child. At that, Jana wouldn't fail.

She turned away from the window. It had seemed simple enough in London. But now she was back and Brandon was different. Warm, caring, kind. Attentive and even a romantic.

Handsome as ever, too.

The thought crept into Jana's mind, but she determinedly pushed it away.

Was Brandon different this time? He *seemed* different. But was he? Really? Perhaps this was all an act to get her to stay with him. Would he go to that trouble? That extreme? Jana didn't know.

Not that it mattered. Even if she threw caution to the wind and decided to stay with Brandon, give their marriage another chance, it was doomed now. Once Brandon found out how she'd kept his child from him, he'd be furious. Any love he felt for Jana would be dashed. He'd send her away. Their marriage would be over. For good, this time.

And what if he wanted to keep her baby?

Revulsion rose in Jana, a wave of anger and terror. Lose her baby? Not see her child again?

Never.

So that left her with no choice but to attempt to ruin Brandon's dearest venture, the Jennings project. He would end their attempted reconciliation. She would leave, taking her baby with her. Brandon would never be the wiser.

Because nothing was more important than her baby.

Chapter Nineteen

Having breakfast with Brandon, seeing him first thing in the morning across the table had become part of their new routine that Jana liked. There was something about him at this early hour. Crisp shirt, freshly shaved, smelling faintly of soap and cotton. More than once Jana had caught herself wanting to reach out and touch his smooth jaw, lean close and get a good whiff.

Yet today, she wished he would revert back to his old ways, just this once. She was dying to learn whether or not Oliver had actually run her women's article and her Ask Mrs. Avery column in the *Messenger*. She wouldn't have been surprised if he'd lost his nerve. Nor would she have blamed him. Brandon would be a formidable enemy.

"Are you going to the refuge this afternoon?" Brandon asked, sipping his coffee.

Jana jumped, visions of today's planned clandestine

rendezvous with Oliver at the refuge jarring her. "Yes, for a little while."

"How is the volunteer list coming along?" he asked.

Was that some hidden meaning in the seemingly innocent question? Jana suddenly thought. Had Brandon somehow learned what she and Oliver were up to?

No, no, of course he couldn't know. She cautioned herself to calm down, lest she give away their plan herself.

"Filling up quickly. Almost everyone I've approached has agreed to volunteer," Jana said. She rushed ahead, anxious to steer the conversation to another topic. "What are you doing today?"

"I'm just about to close the deal on the warehouse purchase," Brandon said. "Once that's handled, I can move on with—"

"Excuse me," Charles intoned from the doorway.

Jana and Brandon both stopped eating and looked up at him. The butler almost never interrupted them at mealtime.

"Your aunt has arrived," he said.

Jana gasped and shot to her feet so quickly the chair almost tipped over. Aunt Maureen was here? Her presence could mean only one thing: something had happened with the baby. A hundred different possibilities raced through Jana's mind. She felt the color drain from her face.

Brandon saw her expression and leaped to his feet. "What is it? What's wrong?"

"Aunt Maureen—something terrible must have happened—"

"What would your aunt be doing here in Los Angeles?" Brandon asked.

"Excuse me," Charles said, raising his voice slightly. "Not *your* aunt, Mrs. Sayer. Mr. Sayer's aunt."

"*My* aunt?"

Stunned, Jana looked up at Brandon. He looked as surprised as she felt. She didn't even know he *had* an aunt. He seemed completely at a loss, as well.

"Who is she?" Jana asked him.

But Brandon had already pushed past her, headed out of the room. Jana followed, her mind flashing to the bundles of correspondence she'd gone through since returning home. Had there been a letter from an aunt advising them of her visit? Had Jana overlooked it?

At the edge of the foyer Jana paused, a little surprised to see Brandon greeting his gray-haired aunt. He looked even taller, more robust standing next to her as they spoke. Around them, two servants carried in trunks, satchels and hat boxes, piling them in the foyer at Charles's direction. A young woman, who appeared to be the aunt's maid, flitted between them.

After a moment, Brandon looked back, saw Jana and waved her over.

"Aunt Rosa, my wife Jana," he said. "Jana, my aunt, Rosa Delaney."

Aunt Rosa, small and a little frail-looking, was impeccably dressed in a gray gown. She seemed a bit befuddled amid the confusion.

"I'm so pleased to meet you," Jana said, putting on her best hostess smile.

"At long last," Rosa said. "Long overdue, Hannah."

"Jana," she said, gently correcting the older woman.

"Charlotte!" Aunt Rosa turned her head left and right. "Charlotte! Where is that girl?"

"Who are you looking for?" Jana asked.

"Why, Charlotte, of course. Where is she? Charlotte!"

A tall, slender young woman walked through the door. She was nicely dressed, her clothing that of the working class.

"Where have you been?" Aunt Rosa demanded.

"Seeing to the luggage, Miss Delaney," she replied and gestured out the front door.

"What? Oh yes, of course. Charlotte is my secretary," Aunt Rosa explained. "Come in here, Charlotte. Meet my nephew Brandon and his wife Hannah."

"Good morning," Charlotte said. She nodded, offering nothing resembling a smile.

"This is quite a surprise," Jana said.

"Nonsense!" Aunt Rosa insisted, then paused. "Charlotte, didn't you send my letter to Brandon?"

"No, Miss Delaney." Charlotte failed miserably at hiding an exasperated sigh, then went on. "As I said both last evening and this morning, you made no plans to visit anyone in Los Angeles."

"Well, of course I did," Aunt Rosa said, dismissing Charlotte's words with a wave of her hand and turning once again to Brandon and Jana. "I'm touring the

West. On my way to San Diego. Meeting friends there, you know."

"At any rate, I'm glad you decided to stop here and see us," Jana said. "How long will we have the pleasure of your company?"

"A few days," Aunt Rosa said. She drew in a breath and looked around, as if taking in her new surroundings. "So good to be off of that train. Private car, and all."

"Please come in," Jana said, gesturing down the hallway, "and have some refreshment."

"Yes, yes, of course," Aunt Rosa said. "Charlotte? Charlotte!"

"I'm right here, Miss Delaney," she replied.

Aunt Rosa twisted her head, finally spotting her secretary amid the clutter of trunks. "Where are we going after this?"

"San Diego, ma'am."

Aunt Rosa eyed her sharply. "San Diego?"

"Yes, ma'am. You're visiting friends there."

The older woman pursed her lips and scrunched her brow for a few seconds, then shook off her thoughts. "I could do with some refreshment," she announced.

Jana exchanged a look with Brandon. He stepped forward and offered his arm to his aunt.

"This way, Aunt Rosa," he said.

She took hold with both hands and gazed up at him. "Good gracious, dear, but I believe you've grown since I last saw you."

Brandon grinned down at the little woman clinging

to his arm. "Probably so, Aunt Rosa," he said as he led her away.

"Charlotte!" she called, not looking back. "See to our things, Charlotte. Hannah will help you."

Charlotte didn't respond, just watched down the hallway as the two of them disappeared into the sitting room.

She turned to Jana. "Please accept my apology for this intrusion, Mrs. Sayer. Our train arrived in the city last evening, as scheduled, and Miss Delaney suddenly insisted that she would visit her nephew. I explained to her that no arrangements had been made and it was unthinkable to simply drop by. She gets confused. As with your name. I've told her it isn't Hannah, but—"

"It's all right," Jana said and truly meant it. She could see Charlotte had her hands full with Brandon's aunt.

"I doubt we'll be here longer than a few days," Charlotte said. "She's meeting friends in San Diego. They're expecting her."

"Fine," Jana said. "Let's get all of you settled."

She spoke with Charles and instructed him to have the maids freshen rooms for Aunt Rosa's servants, and to prepare a chamber for Aunt Rosa herself. Since redecorating on the second floor was still underway, only one bedchamber was fit for company. She went to the kitchen then and advised Mrs. Boone that unexpected guests had arrived. Thankfully, the cook nodded briskly and put her assistants to work right away.

In the sitting room, Jana found Aunt Rosa seated on

the settee and Brandon standing at the fireplace, his elbow resting on the marble mantel shelf. She paused in the doorway for a moment, studying the two of them. Despite Aunt Rosa's aged features, the hint of a family resemblance was evident. It caused a little chill to slide up Jana's spine.

She'd never met any of Brandon's family. None of them had traveled from New York to San Francisco for their wedding. Jana had thought it odd, but Brandon had explained that his grandfather's health wasn't good and he couldn't make the trip. The dozens of friends and business associates who'd attended more than made up for Brandon's lack of family.

Now, seeing Brandon looking decidedly uncomfortable with his aunt's presence, Jana wondered if perhaps something else was going on.

Her heart sank a little. The man was her husband and all she knew of his family was what had been reported to Aunt Maureen by a private detective.

What a terrible wife she'd been to him.

Brandon straightened away from the fireplace when Jana walked into the room, and she wasn't sure if he was relieved—or troubled—by her presence.

"So, Aunt Rosa, you're Brandon's aunt?" Jana asked, settling herself into the wingback chair across from her. She wondered if Rosa was actually a cousin or some other distant relative who'd taken the title of "aunt" simply because of her age.

"Brandon's grandfather, Winston, is my brother,"

Aunt Rosa said. "So, actually, that makes me Brandon's great-aunt."

"You're the first relative of Brandon's that I've met," Jana said. "On either side of his family."

Aunt Rosa pursed her lips. "You certainly wouldn't have met anyone on the *Sayer* side of the family."

"How was your journey?" Brandon asked.

Jana glanced at him. Had he noted the distaste in Aunt Rosa's voice at the mention of his father's name? Or was it Jana's imagination?

"Delightful," she declared. "I'm touring the West. I especially want to see California."

"This is California," Jana said gently.

"Good, then. I want to see it." Aunt Rosa turned to Brandon. "Your grandfather sends his best."

"Too bad he couldn't make the trip with you," Jana said. "I'd really enjoy meeting him."

"Winston is much too busy, much too busy," Aunt Rosa said.

"At least he's well enough to travel," Jana said.

"Well enough?" Aunt Rosa's brows rose. "That man has never had an ill day in his life."

Jana glanced at Brandon. "But I thought—"

"How's the rest of the family?" Brandon asked.

"Quite well, of course…I suppose…actually, I haven't really seen them in a while." Aunt Rosa frowned, as if trying to remember. Then she shook off the effort. "I'm sure they're all just fine."

Charles appeared in the doorway and nodded discreetly to Jana, signaling that the guest room had been prepared.

"After you're settled," Jana said, getting to her feet, "I'll be happy to show you around the city."

"Excellent," Aunt Rosa declared, rising from the settee with a little effort.

"We'll spend the day together and get acquainted," Jana said. "I know a perfect spot for luncheon. We can—"

"I'll go with you," Brandon offered.

Jana's brows bobbed upward. "You want to go along?" she asked, hearing the surprise in her own voice.

"Sure," he said.

She'd thought her offer to escort Aunt Rosa around the city today would be a favor to Brandon. He hardly had the patience for sitting in a carriage all day, rolling past sights he'd seen hundreds of times—even if their guest was a family member he surely hadn't seen in years.

"But what about your work?" she asked. "You mentioned your warehouse purchase at breakfast. Don't you have to conclude the deal today?"

He shrugged. "It can wait."

It can wait? Jana's eyes widened and her jaw fell open. Brandon actually intended to put off a business transaction? Could he really be that desperate to see his aunt?

Jana doubted it. Something else was going on. She was almost certain she saw his mind working, mulling over something.

"I plan to take Aunt Rosa to the tearoom for luncheon," Jana warned him.

"That bird tearoom?" He cringed slightly. "Quail? Pheasant? Turkey?"

"The Peacock Tea Room," Jana said. "I know it's not exactly one of your favorite spots, but—"

"No, it's fine. We'll go there."

Now she knew something was up.

But Brandon gave her no chance to ask anything further. He turned to his aunt.

"We'll leave as soon as you're ready," he said.

"Well, then, let's get on with it," Aunt Rosa declared. "Charlotte? Charlotte!"

A few minutes later, the secretary entered the sitting room. Jana explained their plans for the day and Charlotte did an admirable job of not looking relieved at hearing that Rosa would be occupied elsewhere for hours.

"We'll leave as soon as you've freshened up," Jana said.

"We won't be long," Charlotte answered as she escorted Rosa out of the sitting room.

"You really don't have to go, Brandon," Jana said. "I know how important that warehouse purchase is to you."

He shook his head. "I want to go. I'll place a telephone call to the office and tell Perkins that I won't be in today. He'll handle everything."

"All right. If you're sure."

Brandon didn't answer, but he did move closer, so

close they nearly touched. He glanced at the doorway, then leaned down a little and lowered his voice.

"There is something I'd like to talk to you about."

An odd feeling crept over Jana. She wasn't certain if Brandon's words brought it on—or his closeness.

"Could we go someplace…private?" he whispered.

His breath puffed against her ear. Jana fought off a shiver.

"Well, all right," she said, wondering if that was a wise idea.

Brandon nodded and left the room, leaving her to follow. They wound through the house, past the crew already at work this morning in the parlor and his study. Most of the major construction had been completed, cutting down on the noise of the hammers and saws. Now they busied themselves with the detail work.

When they reached the little storage room near the kitchen that Jana had designated Brandon's new study, he motioned her inside, then followed. With the desk, chair and sidetable already wedged inside, hardly any room was left for the two of them. Brandon pulled the door closed, throwing them into near darkness. Jana gasped as he suddenly pressed his full body against hers. She leaned back, bracing her hands against the desktop. His arm circled her waist, holding her steady.

Her heart raced at the feel of his chest snuggling against her breasts, and his leg easing between her thighs. Good gracious, what was happening?

The overhead light snapped on, filling the room with

feeble light, and Jana found herself gazing up into Brandon's face. They hung there for a few seconds, both frozen in place.

"Just, ah, just turning on the light," Brandon said, keeping her in his grasp.

Jana pulled her gaze from his face and saw that he still held on to the overhead light cord. She shifted, attempting to extricate herself from his grasp, but only succeeded in dragging her breasts across his chest and allowing his thigh to slip deeper between hers.

His gaze dipped to her bosom, and though her dress covered her to her throat, her skin tingled as if he could see straight through the fabric.

Brandon straightened away from her. She backed away and bumped into a wall. In the confines of the room, that left them only a foot or so apart.

"What…what did you want to talk to me about?" Jana asked, smoothing down the skirt of her dress.

His gaze followed her hands, sending another wave of warmth through her.

"Since my aunt is here I thought we should address our situation," Brandon said. "I'd prefer she didn't learn that you and I are having difficulties."

Jana admonished herself for allowing her thoughts to wander. Of course Brandon wouldn't want his aunt to know the truth of their situation, go back home to New York and spill the news to everyone in the family. Jana wasn't anxious to be the topic of the Delaney gossip mill, either.

She drew in a breath, trying to ignore the tingling in her breasts Brandon had caused, and turned her attention to their very real problem.

"You're right," she said. "I'd rather keep this to ourselves."

"Then you're agreeable to us acting as if we're a normal married couple?" he asked, then hastened to add, "In my aunt's presence."

Jana drew back a little. "What, exactly, did you have in mind?"

He shrugged. "When I offer my arm, I'd appreciate it if you'd take it."

That made perfect sense. "Certainly."

"Allow me to assist you in and out of the carriage."

"That's reasonable."

"I think a modest showing of affection would be appropriate," Brandon said. "For instance, if I take your hand."

To demonstrate, he lifted her hand, his big warm fingers closing around hers. He leaned down a little, drawing her hand to his lips.

"A small kiss?" he suggested, then placed his lips on the back of her hand. "Would that be all right?"

Jana gulped. "Y-yes…"

He kissed her softly, then turned her hand and pressed his lips against the soft underside, his tongue gliding over her palm.

Heat surged from her hand, up her arm and over her breasts, then arrowed lower. A moan slipped through her lips.

Brandon's mouth worked its way across her palm, then closed over the end of her finger, his tongue and lips tugging at the tip. Jana's knees weakened, and she pushed back against the wall to keep from falling.

With deliberate slowness, Brandon moved from one finger to the next, working a long-forgotten magic that held Jana breathless.

When he finally lifted his head, he said, "And would it be all right if I smelled your hair?"

He held on to her hand, swirling his thumb against her palm. She couldn't answer.

"I love the smell of your hair," Brandon whispered. "And your neck. That one spot…right below your ear…right here…"

Emotion rose in Jana as Brandon leaned down. She shuddered when his mouth pressed against that particular spot, the one he'd just described…the one she remembered he liked so much, all those months ago. His lips moved over her flesh, then his teeth and his tongue.

Brandon settled both hands at her waist, pulling her just a little closer. He lifted them slowly until his thumbs brushed the underside of her breasts. Jana leaned her head sideways, unable not to, giving him better access to her neck.

He cupped her breasts, kneading them gently. Jana shifted, pushing them farther into his hands. His thumbs moved higher and higher, and her nipples tightened in anticipation, suddenly anxious for his touch.

But he stopped short and lifted his head.

"I don't think we should do this in front of my aunt," he said softly, his hands still on her.

Jana just looked at him, too befuddled by his caress to make any sense out of his words.

"Should we?" he asked again.

The sensual fog in her brain cleared a little, leaving Jana to understand what he was saying. But before she could answer him, he started in again.

His hands stroked her breasts. His thumbs turned in big circles, circles that grew smaller and smaller until—finally—they skimmed the crest.

Jana gasped and pressed herself against him.

But he backed away, his fingers remaining long enough to caress her breasts once more.

"I think we're in agreement on everything," he said.

"Wh-what?" she stammered, her body aching with unfulfilled need.

"We're in agreement on how to act in front of my aunt." Brandon gave her a quick nod and opened the door. "I'll meet you in the foyer."

Then he disappeared. A swirl of fresh air rushed into the room, but did little to cool Jana.

After this, she had to spend the afternoon with Brandon—and his aunt along as chaperone?

How would she ever manage?

Chapter Twenty

By the time the three of them returned home that evening, Aunt Rosa—oddly enough—seemed to be the only one with energy to spare.

"Quite a day, yes, quite a day," Aunt Rosa declared as they entered the house.

"I'm glad you enjoyed it," Jana said, managing to put some enthusiasm into her voice.

"The West is beautiful," she said. "I can't wait to see California."

Jana didn't bother to correct her.

The unlikely trio had covered much of the city today by carriage, with Brandon playing the role of tour guide. He pointed out things of interest, many of them Jana herself hadn't known about, some she remembered from the first three months of their marriage.

After lunch at the tearoom, Aunt Rosa had wanted to visit some of the stores along Wilshire Boulevard, so they'd set out on foot. She'd fawned over nearly everything she laid eyes on, and bought gifts to send to this or that friend, or a relative Jana had never heard of.

The woman's bouts of senility presented themselves often, and Jana had to remind her several times that she'd already purchased the exact same gift. Aunt Rosa wandered off twice.

The whole day left Jana exhausted.

Brandon, surely, was worn out from staring at her breasts all day. Each time he spoke to her, every time she glanced his way, his gaze rested on her bosom. He hadn't made eye contact with her all day. She doubted he could describe the style of hat she wore today if his life depended on it.

When they passed the Bradbury Building that housed Brandon's office, she half expected him to ask the driver to stop so he could run in and see how things were going. She almost wished that he would. His constant attention to her bustline reminded her over and over again of their escapade in the storage room this morning.

The only respite Jana received all day was their brief stop at the women's refuge. While Brandon gave his aunt a tour of the facility, Jana had interrupted Oliver Fisk's tutoring session and, behind the closed door of the office, passed along the article and Ask Mrs. Avery column she'd written last night. Much to her relief, he'd told her that the first articles and column had run in the morning paper. She made him promise they would continue.

"Are you ready for supper?" Jana asked as they crossed the foyer, silent hoping the woman would say no.

"Supper in my room, I think. Charlotte!"

"I'll have Cook send up a tray," Jana told her.

"Yes, that will be fine." Aunt Rosa drew herself up and turned to Brandon. "So, what do you recommend for tomorrow?"

"What would you like to see?" he asked.

"Charlotte! The ocean. And I want to see some of those orange trees one hears so much about. Charlotte! Then Hannah and I can finish up our shopping."

Brandon nodded. "We'll make a day of it."

Jana pressed her lips together to keep from moaning. She couldn't take another full day of Aunt Rosa—or Brandon, for that matter, and his constant attention to her breasts. Every time he *looked* at them, it made her wish he'd *touch* them.

"Let me walk you upstairs," Brandon offered.

"You go ahead," Aunt Rosa said. "I need to go over a few things with Charlotte. Charlotte!"

Jana took the opportunity to dash up the stairs and into the sanctity of her bedchamber. She fell back against the door and heaved a sigh of relief. Quiet. Solitude. At last.

She went into her bathroom, anxious for a long, hot soak in the tub. Abbie came in a few minutes later, helped her undress, then laid out a pale green nightgown and robe and left her in peace. Jana relaxed in the water, letting the heat draw out the ache in her feet and the tension in her neck.

Finally, she dragged herself out of the tub, toweled off and slipped into her night clothes, ready to fall into bed. She knew Abbie would have the coverlet turned down for her.

But when she stepped out of the dressing room, Jana's heart lurched.

Brandon sat at her vanity.

No sign of Abbie.

"What are you doing in here?" Jana demanded.

He selected a bottle from the array on the vanity, pulled out the cork and sniffed.

"Smells good," he said, and sat it down again.

He had on his suit trousers and white shirt, but had left his jacket and cravat on the chair beside her bureau. His sleeves were rolled back and his collar stood open.

"Why are you in here?" Jana asked, walking over.

Brandon sorted through the colorful bottles on her vanity table, picked one up and held it to the light.

"What's this?" he asked.

Jana pulled it from his hand. "I asked you a question," she said.

He gazed up at her and Jana wished she'd kept her mouth shut—and stayed in the bathroom. His line of vision skimmed her face but for an instant, then dipped predictably. She flushed, knowing what Brandon knew—that she wore nothing at all beneath her night-gown and robe.

"Have you forgotten this morning in the storage room?" he asked, his voice low and mellow.

She flushed again, this time feeling the heat spread to her cheeks.

He watched her, waiting. Had he asked her that to remind her of their near tryst this morning? And was that a smug expression on his face?

"Our agreement," Brandon said, providing the answer she couldn't recall, and turning back to the vanity. He selected a cobalt-blue jar and screwed off the lid, then looked up at her once more. "To behave as man and wife during my aunt's visit. Remember?"

Her cheeks flushed. "If you think that our agreement gives you entrance to my bed, you're wrong."

"Who said anything about your bed?" he asked, sniffing the white cream in the jar.

"Well—" She stopped, embarrassment crowding out her simmering annoyance.

"What's this stuff?" he asked, holding up the jar.

"It's a skin softener," she told him. "And what has your aunt and our agreement got to do with you being in here?"

"Her room is right across the hall," Brandon said, putting down the jar. "I walked her upstairs just now. What would she have thought if she'd seen me go into my own bedchamber, instead of yours?"

"I doubt she'd have noticed," Jana insisted.

"She noticed," Brandon assured her. He lifted a green atomizer with a feather sticking out of the top. "What's this?"

"Perfume." Jana plucked it from his hand and put it

back on the vanity table. "Fine. She saw you come in here. Why haven't you left yet?"

Brandon raised an eyebrow. "And have her think I made love to you like a jackrabbit, then abandoned you?"

Her cheeks flamed. "Brandon, really…"

"It's a reflection of your lovemaking too, Jana," he informed her.

Her expression soured. "Is that so?"

"Do you want her to think you're one of those wives who stares at the ceiling, counting backward until the deed is done?" Brandon's eyes darkened. "Especially when you and I both know that's not the case."

"You could go into your room through the connecting door," Jana pointed out, gesturing to the door that had remained closed tight since her arrival.

Brandon nodded. "I could do that. But once that door is opened, well, I can't be held accountable if you barge into my room and force yourself on me."

She opened her mouth to protest, but he went on.

"Besides," he said. "If I go into my room, I can't very well fumble around in the dark. And if I turn on the lamp Aunt Rosa will surely see the light beneath the door and—"

"I honestly don't care what your aunt thinks." Jana flung out both arms.

"You should. She's a snoop. The whole family knows it. She slips around the house, spying on people. She's worse than the servants," he told her. "And she's never been married. That's why she's so interested in the sexual encounters of other people. She doesn't hesitate to tell everything she learns."

"Do you expect me to believe anyone takes her ramblings seriously?" Jana asked. "The woman doesn't even know what *state* she's in."

"You should believe what I tell you," Brandon said.

"If she returns home with stories to tell, no one in the family will know she's referring to me," Jana insisted. "They'll think you've remarried someone named Hannah."

"Aunt Rosa enjoys carrying tales," Brandon said. "You know the saying—anyone not *doing* it is *talking* about it."

"Like you?"

"Exactly."

Jana rolled her eyes. "Would you please leave? I'm tired, my feet hurt and I want to go to bed."

"Oh, here then."

Brandon sprang off the vanity bench and dragged over an upholstered chair.

"Sit down," he said.

She didn't move.

He gestured to the bed. "If you'd rather, we can go there and—"

"Never mind." Jana plopped down in the chair.

Brandon straddled the bench, caught her ankle and pulled her foot up between his legs.

"What are you doing?" she demanded, yanking down her nightgown.

"I think you'd enjoy a foot rub," he told her, cupping her ankle with one hand. He gave her a crooked smile. "I think you'd enjoy a great deal more than that, but you'll have to settle for my hands on your feet right now."

"You're certainly full of yourself tonight," she told him, fighting off the warmth of his palm.

"Let's see now," he said, looking over the selection of bottles on the vanity table.

He scooted a little closer to her and Jana's whole leg seemed to ignite knowing what rested against her arch.

"This one should do it." Brandon dipped the thick cream from the cobalt-blue jar and rubbed it between his hands, warming it. He spread it over her feet, rubbing gently, sliding his long fingers between her toes. Jana tried not to relax, tried not to enjoy it. By the time he went to work on her other foot, she gave up the struggle.

She could have let him keep at it all night, but knew it was better if he left. At least, that's what her head told her. The rest of her said something entirely different.

"I'm sure it's safe to leave now."

"You're just going to use me, then send me on my way?" he asked.

"Yes."

"Aren't you going to offer to return the favor?"

"I don't think a foot rub is the favor you'd ask for."

"I might surprise you," he said, looking slightly offended.

"I doubt that."

Brandon lowered her foot gently to the floor, then rose from the bench. "Good night."

"Good night," she said.

He hesitated a moment, then crossed the room and opened the door. He peeked out, then jumped back inside and closed the door.

"Aunt Rosa is in the hallway," he whispered.

"She is not. You're making that up as an excuse to stay here."

"Come see for yourself."

Determined to prove a point, Jana walked over and opened the door a crack. She leaned forward, then gasped as her bottom snuggled against Brandon. Glancing over her shoulder she saw him leaning into her.

"Get off of me," she said.

"I'm just trying to see into the hallway," he said, attempting to look innocent as he stepped back.

Jana glanced outside, then opened the door wider and stepped into the hallway. "There's no one out here."

Brandon ambled out of Jana's room. "I could have sworn I saw Aunt Rosa."

"Good night, Brandon."

She turned to go back into her room, but Brandon stepped in front of her, blocking her path. He eased closer, forcing her against the wall. Gazing down at her, he held her captive with only the look in his eyes.

"I'll be in my room all night," he whispered, "just in case you change your mind and decide to force yourself on me."

"That won't happen," she told him. But even as she spoke the words, her breath grew short as the heat of his body seeped through her thin robe and gown.

"Are you sure?" Brandon touched his finger to the spot behind her ear—the one he'd made such good use of this morning in the storage room—and trailed his finger down her throat to the top button of her robe.

An ache of longing rose in Jana. How she wanted to give in to him, to her own desire. How she wished things could be good between them. That their future could be bright and filled with hope.

But she'd sealed their marriage to doom in London when she'd decided not to tell Brandon about his child. And it was too late to change that now.

She allowed herself one last look at him, then tore away and went into her room, closing the door firmly behind her.

Brandon stared at the door, his body throbbing, fighting against every instinct that urged him to go in after her. If he got her into bed, she'd be his. He'd have her. She wouldn't leave him again. The bond between them would be too strong for her to break.

But that was no way to start their marriage over a second time. Brandon grumbled under his breath as he pushed away from her door and went into his own room.

He'd come up with this idea of getting her into bed, thinking it would solve their problems, but so far the plan only seemed to be working on *him*. He wanted her now even more than before. He was miserable with need, achy from longing, exhausted with desire.

And he was still sleeping alone.

Brandon punched his fist into his open palm. He needed a better plan.

Chapter Twenty-One

After a second day of squiring Aunt Rosa around town, traveling to the ocean and taking in an orange grove, Jana had to press her lips together to keep from cheering when the woman announced at supper that she planned to be on her way the following morning.

"So soon?" Jana asked, trying not to sound excited at the news.

She glanced at Brandon, seated at the far end of the dining table. His expression gave away nothing. Jana had been surprised that he'd spent every moment these past two days with her and his aunt—shopping, driving around in circles, eating delicate sandwiches and sipping tea at restaurants. He hadn't seemed all that close to his aunt, or any of his family, for that matter.

Was he glad she intended to leave because he'd tired of playing the good host, the dutiful nephew? Was he anxious to get back to his office?

Or was it something more? With Brandon, Jana could never be sure.

"I'm off to San Diego," Aunt Rosa said. "Meeting friends there, you know."

"And where to after that?" Brandon asked.

Aunt Rosa's wrinkled brow pulled together. "Somewhere in California, I think."

Jana and Brandon exchanged a look. Aunt Rosa was a trifle difficult to deal with, at times, but at her age that was to be expected. During this past year, one thing Jana had discovered she possessed an unceasing supply of was patience. It pleased her to see that Brandon seemed to have the same—at least where his aunt was concerned.

They finished supper, then retired to the sitting room. Aunt Rosa chatted about the friends she planned to meet in San Diego, how she'd met them, when and where. Jana didn't know the people and Brandon didn't seem to know them either, but they let her talk.

"I'd better retire for the evening," Jana said, after a while.

"Well, yes, of course," Aunt Rosa said. "I suppose I should retire as well."

"Good night, then," Jana said and left the room, leaving Brandon to escort his aunt upstairs.

When she got to her bedchamber, Jana's routine was much the same as the night before. A hot bath, a fresh gown and robe. She wiped steam from the bathroom mirror and studied her reflection. Damp and dewy, her hair up, a few tendrils curling around her neck. Pink cheeks. Moist lips.

Was this the look of a woman who expected to find her husband waiting in her bedchamber?

Last night. Brandon seated at her vanity table. It had been so long since she'd seen him there, strong and sturdy among her delicate, feminine things.

Would he be there again tonight?

Jana pushed the thought—and the little surge of emotion—away and admonished herself. She didn't want Brandon in her bedchamber.

But when she stepped out of her dressing room and saw the empty vanity bench, her heart sank. Disappointment settled in her stomach, and she—

"Enjoy your bath?"

She whirled at the sound of his voice and saw him lying on her bed. Stretched out, propped up on a stack of pillows, his hands behind his head and his ankles crossed, he watched her.

Jana's heart fluttered. "What are you doing in here?"

His gaze caressed her for a moment. "I like seeing you right after your bath. Remember, Jana? Those first three months together? You'd let me brush your hair. Did you like that about us?"

Yes, she remembered. Jana's heart beat a little harder at the recollection. Yet she couldn't tell him how much she had enjoyed those times with him. It would be too cruel…giving him false hope.

"I take it," Jana said, changing the subject, "that your aunt is loose in the house, spying on us."

"I'm sure she is," Brandon said. "But I'm here tonight for something else."

Just what that *something else* might be sprang up between them. Jana's breath caught. Brandon sat up on the bed.

"I wanted to thank you for being such a gracious hostess to my aunt," he said.

Jana relaxed a little at this safe topic of conversation.

"I enjoyed her visit. She's a little trying, at times, but who isn't?" Jana said. "Besides, she's the only member of your family I've ever met."

She thought he might speak up, volunteer something about his relatives in New York, but he didn't.

"So," Brandon said. "Thank you. It was a difficult two days."

"Two days and you didn't go to your office once," Jana said, shaking her head in awe. "I don't remember you ever taking even one day off from your work."

"Yeah. That was damn stupid of me."

His admission startled her. So did the sincerity in his gaze when he looked up at her.

"I did a lot of stupid things. Most of them involved you," he said.

"When I was in London, I thought of you every day."

The confession slipped out before Jana realized what she was saying. But it was true. She'd thought of him because she carried his child. Because she was confused and didn't know what to do. Because she couldn't bear facing the same sort of life with him if she returned home.

Because she feared he'd take her baby from her.

Surprise showed on Brandon's face at her unexpected admission. He rose from the bed, but didn't come any closer.

"I daydreamed that I'd find myself standing at a window," Jana went on, "and suddenly, you'd appear. You'd leap from a carriage, charge up the stairs and take me into your arms, begging for forgiveness. You'd confess that you couldn't live without me and plead with me to return home with you."

"But I didn't," he said, a pained expression on his face.

Jana wasn't sure if it was the memory of his complacency that troubled him, or something else.

Brandon took a step toward her. "I wanted you to come back, Jana. But I couldn't…"

"Couldn't what?" she asked.

He opened his mouth as if he wanted to tell her something, then turned away, no longer meeting her gaze.

She fought the urge to go to him, comfort him, find a way to ease whatever troubled him.

"It was all my fault," she said at last. "I was the one who left. I accepted the consequences of my actions."

They were quiet for a long while, just looking at each other, both lost in thought.

"So what happens next?" Brandon proposed.

Jana shrugged, knowing what she should say—that

her deception dictated that she must leave again. But she couldn't bring herself to tell him.

Or was it that she couldn't fully accept it herself? Did some tiny part of her cling to the hope that somehow, despite everything that had happened between them, everything that she'd done, their problems might work out?

Yet could she really expect him to forgive her? Could any man? And did she have a right to ask for his forgiveness?

"We still have some time left," Jana said. "Our four weeks isn't up."

"So there's still hope?"

"There's always hope," she said. But Jana didn't know how well it would hold up in the face of reality.

From the look on Brandon's face, he shared her unspoken opinion. He walked to the door, then stopped and looked back.

"There must have been something you liked about us, Jana," he said, his voice almost a plea. "Something, surely…"

A lump of emotion rose in her throat. "Good night, Brandon," she whispered.

He left.

The commotion in the foyer proved worse at Aunt Rosa's departure than during her arrival. Her mountain of luggage had nearly doubled due to all the shopping she'd done. Two servants carried piece after piece outside to be loaded into the waiting carriage, while other servants brought more from upstairs. Charles directed their work while Aunt Rosa's maid fretted in the corner. Charlotte went outside to oversee the packing.

Aunt Rosa stopped at the edge of the foyer. "Where *did* all this luggage come from? Charlotte!"

"These are all yours, Aunt Rosa," Brandon assured her.

"Oh, dear," Aunt Rosa said, latching on to Jana's arm. "I'm afraid my maid has packed some of your things. Charlotte!"

"No, really, it's fine," Jana told her. "Remember? You and I went shop—"

"Charlotte!"

"You and I shopped," Jana said, trying again. "You bought gifts for—"

"Charlotte! Where is that girl? There's been a terrible mistake here. Charlotte!"

Concerned now because Aunt Rosa seemed to be genuinely troubled, Jana cast a pleading look at Brandon. He touched his aunt's shoulder gently.

"It's all right," he said. "I'll get Charlotte. Don't worry, Aunt Rosa. I'll take care of everything."

"Oh yes, well, thank you, dear," she said, quieting as he headed out the front door. She looked up at Jana. "He's such a wonderful boy."

Jana smiled. "That's true."

"And so lucky to have found a fine wife like you, Hannah."

"That's kind of you to say," Jana told her, as a pang of guilt stabbed her stomach.

"We were all so worried about him," Aunt Rosa went on. "The trauma, you know."

"About his parents?" Jana asked, realizing suddenly that this was the first time since her arrival that she'd been alone with Aunt Rosa.

The woman shuddered. "It was all so unseemly."

"The death of Brandon's parents?"

"A scandal, really." Aunt Rosa pursed her lips together distastefully. "Of course, no one expected anything of Holly, really."

"Who's Holly?"

"Brandon's mother. And in that regard, she didn't disappoint. But after what happened in Europe…" Aunt Rosa's eyes widened. "Charlotte!"

"Charlotte's coming. What happened in Europe?" Jana asked, struggling to keep her voice level.

"Well, of course, none of us *knew*. Had we known… But to find out from an *outsider*." Aunt Rosa leaned closer to Jana. "She presented herself to be a woman of breeding, but everyone of substance knew Leona Riley was an opportunist."

"Leona?" Jana's heart rose in her throat. "Leona Albright?"

Aunt Rosa shrugged as if she hadn't heard the question. "In Europe, on her second marriage by then, so I understand. And there was Brandon. A child. Only ten years old."

Jana touched her hand to her forehead. "I—I don't understand what you're saying, Aunt Rosa."

"Some liberties simply should not be taken," she replied. "Charlotte! Where is that girl?"

"Brandon is getting her," Jana said. "You were telling me something that happened with Brandon in Europe? With Leona?"

"I was?" Aunt Rosa frowned. "Oh, yes. Of course. Well, my dear, it was a family situation and should have been dealt with as such. Leona had no business—"

"All set." Brandon's voice boomed as he walked through the front door.

Jana gasped. Her gaze flew to him. He stopped abruptly, reading her horrified expression.

Good gracious, what was Aunt Rosa trying to tell her? A family scandal? Involving Brandon—and Leona Albright?

Brandon turned to Aunt Rosa, ignoring Jana.

"Everything's ready," he said, taking his aunt's arm.

Jana trailed behind, responding automatically to Aunt Rosa's thanks. She watched from the doorway as Brandon helped the woman into the carriage, slammed the door and waved as they pulled away.

Seeing him standing in the drive watching the carriage for so long, Jana realized there was a reason Brandon hadn't gone to work these past two days, and it wasn't because he wished to visit with his aunt.

He didn't want his aunt and Jana to be alone together.

And when he'd walked into the house just now and seen the expression on Jana's face, he knew that in those short minutes, Aunt Rosa had told her something Brandon didn't want her to know.

He seldom spoke of his family and had led Jana to believe the memories were too painful to speak of. Perhaps they were. But something more had happened.

Why wouldn't Brandon tell her?

And why had she been such a poor wife that she'd never asked?

Chapter Twenty-Two

The sway of the carriage, the familiar route, certainty about what awaited him, soothed Brandon as he headed toward his office in the Bradbury Building. Like a work-horse returned to the field, the sameness of the situation comforted him.

He'd been away from the office for two days, returning now midmorning on the third. His instructions to his secretary had been heeded. No interruptions. No matter what. Mr. Perkins was a stickler for obeying directives. Two days gone, and Brandon was anxious to return, catch up on things, head off any problems, though he couldn't imagine that anything catastrophic could have happened during his short absence.

Not that taking the two days off had done him any good, in the end. All his efforts, staying home, playing host, gallivanting around the city might have been for naught. Aunt Rosa had told Jana something just before she left this morning; he saw it in her eyes. Brandon didn't know what, exactly, but he could imagine. He'd left the house as soon as Aunt Rosa's carriage pulled away, giving Jana no chance to ask him anything.

Jana... Brandon leaned his elbow against the carriage window and gazed out at the passing buildings, yet not seeing any of them. Jana consumed his thoughts, his sleep, every waking moment.

Last night he had almost convinced himself not to go to her bedchamber. He didn't trust himself to be alone with her. If he touched her again—even her feet—he might give in to temptation.

And he hadn't been able to come up with a better plan to win her heart. Every time he thought about her, his brain shut down and other body parts started working double-time.

A cold chill passed over him, an old ache he'd experienced too many times already.

Jana was going to leave him.

Again.

He knew it.

Brandon swore a mumbled oath. He couldn't let her go. He *couldn't* bear the thought. Some way, somehow, he had to show her that staying with him was the right thing to do. Right for both of them. But how could he reach her? Convince her to stay?

He blew out a heavy breath, pushing the thought to a far corner of his mind with considerable effort. He was going to his office now. A place where he'd always been comfortable, where he knew exactly what was happening and why. He controlled things there. He'd have some normalcy in his life.

As soon as he got to his office.

"Mr. Sayer!"

His secretary leaped to his feet the minute Brandon opened the outer office door, freezing him in midstep.

"Leave! You've got to leave! Quickly!" Mr. Perkins declared, rounding the deck and rushing toward him.

"What the devil's gotten into you, Perkins?" Brandon asked. He'd never seen the man in such a snit. Eyes bulging, hands waving, white as a sheet.

"It's not safe here. *You're* not safe." The elderly secretary caught Brandon's arm and urged him back out the door. In the office adjoining Mr. Perkins's reception area, Brandon saw his other clerical workers turn worried faces his way.

"What the hell…?"

Afraid Perkins might have a stroke, Brandon stepped out into the corridor.

Sunlight shone through the Bradbury's infamous glass ceiling overhead. Offices opened onto an interior balcony that stretched the width of all five of the building's floors. Marble staircases at either end boasted ornately designed railings of wrought iron and polished wood. The walls were gleaming yellow brick. Two birdcage elevators rose toward the roof.

"Get a hold of yourself, man," Brandon said. "What's this all about?"

Perkins clamped his hands onto the door casings, bracing himself, and jerked his gaze left, then right toward the dual staircases.

"It's clear now," Perkins said, in a low, frantic voice. "But you should use the back stairs, just in case."

"I'm not going anywhere until you tell me what the hell is going on here," Brandon told him, struggling to hold on to his patience.

"They were here yesterday. Then again this morning. They insisted—*insisted*—that they be allowed to speak with you." Perkins drew himself up. "But I held firm, Mr. Sayer. I did just as you said. I told them you couldn't be disturbed."

"Who wanted to see me?"

"Then this morning, *another* group of them showed up," Perkins said, his voice rising.

"*Who?*"

"Women!"

Brandon eased back. "Women?"

"Three of them had on *trousers!* In public! Right here in this very building! In this office! At my desk! *Trousers!*"

Brandon gave the little man a shake. "Calm down, Perkins. I can't make head or tail of what you're telling me."

He gasped and drew in a quick breath. "The women—a dozen, at least, of those progressive, modern women—came here, ranting on and on about how it was high time a man rose to the moment, faced the future and showcased the need for social change."

"Who were they talking about?"

"You."

"Me?"

"They went on and on about how you're championing the rights of women, advising them on how to break the chains of oppression, freeing them from the drudgery of cooking and cleaning, opening new opportunities for downtrodden women in the city."

Brandon just stared at Perkins. He'd explained himself, yet Brandon still didn't have the foggiest idea what he was talking about.

"It's the newspaper, sir," Perkins declared, as if reading his thoughts. "The *Messenger*. It's been running articles for three days now and—"

Perkins froze, his gaze darting up and down the hallway once more. "They're back. That bunch from yesterday. I hear them coming."

Brandon, too, heard the rustle of skirts, the murmur of women's voices and the shuffle of shoes rising from the staircase at the west end of the building.

Perkins pushed up his chin and stepped in front of Brandon, spreading his arms. "Run, Mr. Sayer. I'll hold them off as long as I can."

"Christ…" Brandon gently hustled Mr. Perkins back into the office. But when he saw the women reach the top of the stairs, he steeled himself.

A dozen women—none under the age of forty—steamed toward him. Big hats, and bigger hips. Each wore a scowl and clutched a rolled-up newspaper.

"Ah-ha!" The woman in the lead—Mrs. Fitzpatrick, if he wasn't mistaken, a pillar of the First Methodist Church off Central Square—pointed her newspaper at him and picked up the pace. The others clipped along behind her.

Brandon fell back a step.

"Mr. Sayer. There you are." Mrs. Fitzpatrick planted herself in front of him and the other women fanned out in a semicircle, hemming him against the wall.

"This is an outrage," Mrs. Fitzpatrick declared, holding up the newspaper as if it was a hammer and she was ready—and anxious—to strike a blow. "Decent, God-fearing, church-going people will not tolerate these sorts of actions from you, Mr. Sayer."

"Mrs. Fitzpatrick," Brandon said, glancing uneasily at the women, "I don't understand—"

"You don't understand? You don't understand why your Ask Mrs. Avery column is a scandal?" she demanded.

"My—what?"

"It's a disgrace, an affront to the decent people of this city."

A murmur went through the crowd of women.

"We're appalled, Mr. Sayer, by this unseemly advice given out by your Mrs. Avery," Mrs. Fitzpatrick told him, shaking the newspaper. "Addressing the subject of adultery. Unchristian-like behavior. Appealing to baser instincts. It's shameful."

"I—"

"Who is this woman? This Mrs. Avery?"

Brandon didn't know, but he sure as hell intended to find out.

"I understand your concerns," he said contritely, nodding to all the women pressing in around him. He'd say most anything to send them on their way so he could get to the bottom of this. "As the owner of the newspaper, I assure each and every one of you that I will look into the matter immediately."

"See that you do." Mrs. Fitzpatrick stormed away, the other women giving him one final scathing glare before following.

Brandon pressed his palm to his forehead. Christ, what had happened in the two days he'd been away. And what the hell was Fisk up to at the *Messenger*? He intended to find out.

But as he headed toward the stairway, office doors opened and out stepped several businessmen, all of them Brandon knew. He suspected they'd been hiding in their offices until the women left.

Not that he blamed them.

"See here now, Sayer," Owen Franklin said. "We've got no problem with you pulling that newspaper of yours out of the red."

Around him, heads nodded.

"But hell, man, what are you thinking running those sorts of articles in the *Messenger?*" Franklin demanded. "What are you trying to do to us?"

"After reading your newspaper, my wife is wanting to know how much money I have," another man called out.

"Mine, too," someone else said. "And she wants a say in where it's spent."

"Mine thinks she should have money of her own," a man near the back called out.

"Rayburn down at the California Bank and Trust told me that yesterday two women came in demanding an accounting of their husbands' money," someone else added.

A round of grumbles went through the gathering.

"We can't have this sort of thing going on," Franklin said. "Women walking into our banks. Asking about finances? Hell, what will they want next?"

A chorus of agreement rose from the men

"You'd better do something about this, Sayer," Franklin told him. "And fast."

With a few departing cold stares, the men moved back down the hallway into their own offices. One remained. Noah Carmichael. Brandon hadn't noticed him in the group.

"How the hell could you do this, Brandon?" Noah asked, holding a copy of the newspaper. He sounded hurt and confused and angry. "We're supposed to be partners."

Brandon shook his head. "I don't know what's going on, Noah."

"Where have you been for the last two days? Your newspaper is the talk of the city. Fisk says the presses haven't stopped rolling. The newsboys are frantic.

There's a line outside the newspaper building, waiting for the latest edition. Fisk can barely keep up with the demand."

"Because of a few articles?" Brandon asked. It hardly seemed possible.

"Our Jennings project is ruined," Noah said, his words cold and empty.

Brandon's stomach clenched. "Christ..."

"We've accepted lease fees, shelled out money for architects and construction crews," Noah told him. "I'll lose a fortune on this deal. Not to mention the blow to my business reputation."

"I'll get to the bottom of this," Brandon said. "I promise you that."

But Noah wouldn't let it go so easily. "I've got a wife, Brandon, and a baby on the way. How could you do this to me?"

"Noah, I—"

But he didn't wait for an answer. Noah slapped the newspaper against Brandon's chest, walked back into his office and slammed the door.

Brandon stood in the silent hallway, stunned. He looked down at the newspaper Noah had thrust at him.

How could a few articles and an advice column—all aimed at women, apparently—cause such a stir among so many people? Raise the ire of the ladies of the First Methodist Church to the point of frightening poor old Mr. Perkins? Worry his business associates that their wives might actually want a say in their finances?

And turn his friend against him.

Brandon opened the newspaper and read the articles. "Holy…"

He gulped, then turned to the Ask Mrs. Avery advice column.

"Dammit…" When he got his hands on Oliver Fisk, he was going to kill him.

Brandon headed for the staircase.

Chapter Twenty-Three

"Pssst. Mrs. Sayer?"

Jana jumped as she stepped into the office of the women's refuge and whirled to see Oliver Fisk cowering in the corner.

"Good gracious, Oliver, you startled me," she said, heaving a sign of relief. "And what are you doing in here? Hiding?"

"Shhh." Oliver rushed forward and closed the office door. "You—of all people—should understand."

"Oh. Yes." Jana put down her little satchel and unpinned her hat. "The newspaper."

"This is a fiasco. We have to stop running those articles," he pleaded.

"Stop running them?" Jana laid her hat on the corner cabinet. "Are you serious?"

"Yes," he insisted.

Oliver fidgeted worse than usual, adjusting his spectacles, straightening his jacket, tugging down on his shirtsleeves. He looked wild-eyed and frantic, on the verge of an all-out fit.

"Why do you want to stop?" Jana asked.

"Because we have to. The whole city is in an uproar. Those modern, progressive types are lining up against the women from the church. The men are up in arms. I've received all sorts of complaints these last few days. Demands that I quit publishing the articles, demands that I don't quit. I had to sneak out the back door of the newspaper building to get over here."

"The articles and the Ask Mrs. Avery column are the talk of the town," Jana agreed.

Before coming to the refuge today she'd had lunch with several friends at the tearoom. The women had talked of nothing but the controversial articles. Women at an adjoining table had broken into their conversation, voicing their own opinions. Jana had forced herself to join in, so as not to draw suspicion.

"Everyone is dying to know who this Mrs. Avery is," Jana said. "There's all sorts of speculation."

"The church ladies demanded that I reveal her true identity." Oliver's eyes widened. "I think they intend to do me harm."

"What about the women here at the refuge?" Jana asked. "Do they suspect anything?"

"No," Oliver said. "But they cheered—actually cheered—when I stopped by here yesterday. Then they refused to even look at *Travels with a Donkey in the*

Cevennes—a fascinating book—and insisted they read the *Messenger* instead."

"They cheered my article on proper table settings?" Jana asked.

"It was the Mrs. Avery questions regarding what to do when one suspected her husband of adultery, how to handle a nosy neighbor, dealing with meddlesome in-laws."

Jana sank into the chair behind her desk.

"How are the advertisers handling this?" she asked.

"We've lost a few," Oliver said, "but we've picked up a half-dozen new ones."

"Circulation?"

"We topped the *Times* yesterday for the first time ever. But this—this is a complete disaster." Oliver collapsed into the chair in front of the desk. "It's awful... just awful. I'd—well, I'd wanted to ask Audrey if I could call on her, and now she won't have a thing to do with me."

"She won't?" Jana asked.

"Well, she probably won't," Oliver admitted. "But after my newspaper has instigated this bedlam, why would she?"

"Don't judge Audrey too soon," Jana told her. "She just might find that sort of behavior very alluring."

Oliver's cheeks flushed, then he shook his head. "I'm no rebel. No social reformer. No crusader."

"Perhaps you should be," Jana suggested.

Oliver's eyes widened. "Do you...do you think I could?"

"Of course you could. The stir the newspaper has caused in only three days points up the need for these topics to be addressed. Change is inevitable."

"Well, I suppose…"

Jana opened her satchel and handed him several pieces of paper. "Tomorrow's articles, and the Ask Mrs. Avery column."

"Don't bother making up your own questions any longer." Oliver rose from his chair and fetched his satchel from the corner. He flipped it open on the desk. Out poured dozens of envelopes. "Questions from your public, Mrs. Avery. They've flooded our mail chute."

Jana picked up several of them. "We have to be very careful, Oliver. Keeping Mrs. Avery's true identity a secret will perpetuate the mystique of the column, ensure that circulation continues to rise."

"Not to mention that your husband will kill me if he finds out." Oliver stuffed the papers Jana had given him into his satchel. "I'd better get back to the office."

"Why not wait around?" Jana suggested. "Audrey's supposed to be here in a bit."

Oliver winced. "No…no, I can't face her," he said, and left the office, closing the door quietly behind him.

Jana opened several of the Mrs. Avery questions and read them over. Problems with husbands, mostly.

She had her own husband-problems to deal with. As Oliver had said, Brandon wouldn't be happy when he learned that she was behind the newspaper articles and column. Even though that had been her plan all along, she hadn't anticipated dragging the entire city into a debate on the need for social reform.

Was this another bad decision on her part? Jana wondered. She'd made several already—all of which she'd come to regret. Leaving Brandon in the first place. Running off to Europe. Keeping the baby a secret from him. Not telling him immediately upon her return.

Those choices had all impacted Brandon's life, as well as hers. Now here was another one. As owner of the newspaper, he'd bear the brunt of much of the public outcry over the *Messenger*'s content.

But Brandon had made his share of poor decisions, too. He'd ignored her as a bride, hadn't come after her when she left. He hadn't even written to her. And when she finally returned, he made no effort to change, at first. He had simply wanted to pick up where they'd left off— despite the fact that those very situations had caused her to leave in the first place.

And he had lied to her about his family, about his past. That hurt Jana as much as everything else. Aunt Rosa had unknowingly given him away. Her cryptic comments this morning were troubling, too. Jana wasn't sure if she should confront Brandon, or wait until he chose to tell her. Surely there was a reason for his secrecy.

Did Leona Albright figure into the situation? The idea bothered Jana considerably.

She pushed herself to her feet and shoved the dozens of Mrs. Avery letters into her satchel. Her head had started to hurt and she needed some air. Reaching for her hat, Jana decided she'd go to the Morgan Hotel and visit Aunt Maureen. And the baby, of course. Seeing those bright eyes and that happy smile always lifted her spirits.

Yes, she'd got to the hotel. Nothing bad ever happened there.

Brandon paced the parlor of Leona Albright's Bunker Hill mansion, a home left to her by her second—or was it her third?—husband. Brandon had been here a few times before when Leona had given parties for whatever cause she championed at that particular moment. He didn't remember the parlor looking like this, burnt oranges, creams and deep green colors. What was it with women and decorating all the time?

Brandon had tried to find Oliver Fisk, but he wasn't at the newspaper office. Brandon's instinct was to come here next.

"Why, Brandon darling, what a pleasant surprise," Leona purred as she swept into the room.

Brandon didn't doubt for a minute that Leona would agree to see him, even though calling unannounced was frowned upon. She wore a plum dress, the color complementing her fiery hair.

Leona stopped and tilted her head. "Is that a frown? A frown from the man responsible for a most scintillating scandal?"

He grumbled under his breath. "You've heard, huh?"

"Of course, Brandon. Why, this is even more salacious than when your wife left you."

"Thanks a lot."

"You should be rewarded, actually. Thanks to your newspaper, all the parties have finally gotten interesting."

"I'm looking for Fisk," Brandon said. "Do you know where he is?"

"Why would you think I'd know?" Leona asked, drifting across the room and settling onto the settee.

"A hunch," Brandon told her.

"I've had the pleasure of Oliver's company on a few occasions lately." Leona gave him a little smile. "But not today. Not yet, anyway."

"It's *you*," Brandon realized, the idea hitting him hard. "You're Mrs. Avery. You and Fisk are in cahoots over this whole thing."

She raised a brow. "I'm flattered. But why on earth would you think that?"

"Because Oliver Fisk hasn't got guts enough to pull off something like this," Brandon said.

"Don't be so quick to judge," Leona said, favoring him with a secretive smile. "There's more to Ollie than you realize."

"What's going on with you two?" Brandon demanded.

"Are you asking me to declare my intentions?"

"He strikes me as a little...innocent," Brandon said. "And I heard he's got his eye on a young woman."

"A young, innocent woman?"

"I don't know personally," Brandon said, "but it seems so."

"Then she'll thank me for my effort, one of these days." Leona smiled. "My interest in the dear boy is purely business. I find myself fascinated by the newspaper game."

"Since when?"

"Since I met Oliver."

"You're just amusing yourself."

"He'll be amused too," Leona predicted. "If I choose to invite him over for…tea…one afternoon."

"He'll need some amusement," Brandon grumbled, "after I get my hands on him. The whole city is in turmoil because of what he did."

"What did you expect?" Leona proposed. "You pushed him. You threatened to close his newspaper. Did you think Oliver would lie down and take it?"

"I explained to him what was at stake," Brandon insisted. "I gave him ample warning."

"People do drastic things when they're pushed. You, of all people, should know that."

Brandon glared at her, not answering. Not anxious to admit—if only to himself—that she might be right.

"My Jennings project is ruined," he said, after a moment.

A little frown crossed Leona's face. "With the newspaper flourishing, you can't close it, can you? Can't take over the building. Oh, well. You're a smart man, Brandon. I'm sure you'll figure something out."

"Your confidence is overwhelming," Brandon told her.

"And when you see Oliver, tell him to come by, would you?" She smiled. "I think he could use a serving of my afternoon…tea…right about now."

"Leona, stay away from him."

"You're so cranky." She tsked, then gave him a sultry smile. "Perhaps you should toddle on home and see what your own wife is serving this afternoon."

"Goodbye, Leona."

Brandon stomped out of the house, not bothering to listen for her reply.

Outside, he sent his carriage away without him, preferring to walk off his pent-up energy. If he saw Oliver Fisk right now he just might do him bodily harm. And even though Brandon had wanted to hit someone for a while now, Fisk wouldn't likely stand up to the blow.

Leona's words floated through Brandon's mind as he walked. Go home to his wife. The notion was comforting, surprisingly so. Even though the house was still under construction and he faced a future with a lilac-colored study, the idea of being there warmed him.

Walking in. Seeing Jana. Smelling her sweet scent. Having her tell him everything she'd done today. All that awaited him.

In his mind, Brandon extended the daydream to include whisking her upstairs, the two of them making love all afternoon. He knew it wouldn't happen, even though he'd attempted to woo her a dozen ways.

He could always beg. He hadn't tried that yet.

Brandon pushed on, weaving through pedestrians, crossing streets, dodging the trolley. Somehow, he would have to figure a way to fix this mess Oliver Fisk had gotten him into. The church ladies breathing down his neck, his Jennings project in shambles, loss of considerable money, and his friend turned against him. He could always—

A familiar figure caught Brandon's attention. He turned sharply, staring over the heads of the people crowded around him on the sidewalk.

Jana. Walking into the Morgan Hotel.

Chapter Twenty-Four

Brandon hurried through the crowd of pedestrians on the sidewalk and went inside the Morgan, all the while telling himself there was a perfectly good reason for Jana to be here. At a hotel. In the middle of the day.

Not long ago, Noah had mentioned that he'd seen her at this same hotel. Brandon had figured she was here for a luncheon. He'd even asked her about it.

Jana had answered his questions that day, but he'd wondered if she was holding something back.

And now she was here again.

Brandon paused in the doorway, watching as she crossed the lobby. She looked small amid the gigantic marble columns, the Oriental carpets and low-hanging chandeliers. Guests sat on the plush furnishings and milled around at the registration desk. Bellhops in blue uniforms, loaded down with baggage, hustled toward the wide staircase that led to the rooms upstairs.

Brandon's heart rose to his throat as he watched Jana pause at the bottom step, lift the hem of her dark blue dress, and begin to climb.

Up the stairs. To the guest rooms.

For a moment, he stood there, paralyzed. He couldn't move. He couldn't think. Couldn't understand what he was seeing. Why would Jana be here except to…

Anger surged through Brandon. He crossed the lobby with powerful strides and stopped at the bottom of the staircase.

"Jana!"

Halfway up the stairs she stopped, turned and looked down at him. Brandon saw the shocked expression on her face. His anger doubled.

"What the hell are you doing here!" he demanded.

Jana stood on the step for another few seconds, and he wondered if she would come down to him.

Or continue upstairs.

Then slowly, deliberately, Jana walked down the steps.

She looked up at him. "Perhaps you could speak a little louder, Brandon, I don't think *everyone* heard you."

He didn't give a damn who heard him, but he was certain heads had turned their way.

"Where are you going?" he asked, gesturing up the staircase. He lowered his voice but couldn't take the edge off of it.

Jana gazed at him with that new wealth of patience she'd developed during their time apart. She didn't tear up, didn't break down.

"I'll show you," she said calmly.

But instead of heading up the staircase again, Jana crossed the lobby to the registration desk. Brandon followed.

"Good afternoon, Mrs. Sayer," the young man behind the desk said, all smiles, anxious to please.

"Good afternoon," she answered. "Would you please inform my husband here of the name of the party registered in your finest suite."

The young man cast a troubled glance at Brandon.

"You are, of course, Mrs. Sayer," he reported. "And Miss Maureen Armstrong."

"Thank you," Jana said, and moved away from the desk.

Brandon stared after her, his emotions churning, but for a different reason now. He caught up with her behind one of the marble columns near the entrance.

"Your aunt has been here all this time?" he asked.

Jana nodded. "Yes."

"Waiting?" Brandon demanded, the sense of betrayal knifing through his heart.

"Yes."

"You said you'd honestly try and work things out in our marriage, Jana. You gave me your word. You made a commitment to me." He waved his hand, gesturing at the upper floors. "What the hell is this? Plan B?"

Again, Jana didn't rise to his anger. "I didn't set out to hurt you, Brandon."

But it did hurt, knowing that her aunt was a short

carriage ride from home, ready to take her away from him. Again.

"I've kept things from you, Brandon," Jana said. "But you've done the same. When—and if—you want to talk, I'll be at home."

She ducked around him and left the hotel.

Jana's heart lurched as she heard a familiar voice drifting into the sitting room from the foyer. After their confrontation in the lobby of the Morgan, she wasn't sure whether Brandon would come home at all this evening.

She rose from the settee and watched the doorway, waiting for him to walk through. He'd looked so hurt this afternoon when he'd discovered her at the hotel. She saw in his expression that he suspected her of frequenting the hotel for a love affair. But when she'd revealed to him that Aunt Maureen was the real reason for her visit, he wasn't relieved at all. If anything, he'd been more upset.

She'd made yet another bad decision.

She'd hurt Brandon again.

She'd challenged him, also, to come home this evening and explain his own secretive past. Jana wondered if she'd pushed him too hard. Would this, too, prove to be another bad choice on her part?

She couldn't tell from his expression as he stepped into the doorway of the sitting room. He looked tired, drained, a little pale. Was it from dealing with the newspaper problems? Or coming home feeling he had to confess something he never wanted her to know?

Brandon lingered near the door for a few minutes, then drifted into the room. He watched her, waiting, she supposed, for her to begin their conversation. It seemed only fair.

"Aunt Maureen accompanied me back from London," Jana began. "I asked her to come here with me while I spoke with you about a divorce. I didn't think you'd refuse me, after I'd been away for so long—"

"You thought I didn't love you anymore?" he asked, frowning, looking hurt.

"I didn't know what to think," Jana said. "But it never occurred to me that you'd insist I stay with you for a month and try to rekindle our marriage. Since Aunt Maureen was already here, already settled at the Morgan, she agreed to stay until you and I had decided things one way or the other."

Brandon nodded slowly, as if her explanation made sense and he understood, but was still hurt by it.

"Is there anything more you want to know?" Jana asked.

He met her gaze then. "Are you involved with a man there? Is your aunt covering for you?"

Jana shook her head. "No, Brandon. There's never been any man in my life but you."

He looked at her for another moment, then nodded, apparently satisfied that she'd told him the truth.

"At the hotel I asked you about your secretive past,"

Jana said. "Aunt Rosa mentioned some things that contradicted what you'd told me. She alluded to some problems when you were young."

Brandon shrank back a little and glanced away.

"But you don't have to tell me anything, Brandon, if you don't want to. It's your private business, and if it's too painful to share, then that's fine."

He walked to the window and gazed out at the rear lawn. Shadows stretched across the grounds in the fading light.

"I owe you an explanation for why I never came for you in London," he said.

Jana wasn't sure how the two things connected, but she didn't say anything. Brandon remained at the window, gazing out. She saw him in profile, his face drawn in tense lines.

"My mother was quite a hellion, according to my grandfather," Brandon said. "Rebellious, headstrong. Determined to do just the opposite of anything he told her to do. At age fifteen, just to spite Grandfather, she eloped with a man who was quite beneath the family standards."

"Your father?" Jana asked.

"Yes," Brandon said, still looking out the window. "Grandfather was furious. He forbade her to enter his house, and cut her off without a cent."

"That seems awfully vindictive."

Brandon glanced back at her. "He was as headstrong as she."

"What happened to them?"

"They ended up in Europe, somehow," Brandon said, turning toward the window once again. "In short order, my father disappeared, I was born and my mother was left to fend for herself."

"Your father isn't really dead?" Jana asked.

Brandon lifted his shoulders. "I have no idea what happened to the man."

"What about your mother? How did she get back home from Europe?"

"She didn't. She refused to contact my grandfather and ask for forgiveness or help. Too much pride." Brandon looked back at her once more. "Recognize the family trait?"

She did, but chose not to say so.

"It must have been difficult for your mother making a living on her own and caring for a child."

Brandon drew in a breath and let it out slowly. "No. Not really."

He'd said it easily enough, but the shift of his shoulders, the tightening of his jaw told Jana there was more.

"How did she manage?" she asked slowly, softly, fearing she was asking Brandon to reveal a very ugly truth about his own mother.

"She was young and pretty and vivacious," he said. "And she still had the Delaney family name to trade on. She knew people all over Europe, wealthy people who didn't know she'd been cut off, or caused a scandal. People who wished to garner favors from a member of the

Delaney family. People who welcomed her as one of their own."

"They took the two of you in?"

"No."

A few minutes passed, so many that Jana wondered if he intended to go on with the story. She let him take his time.

Brandon braced his hand against the windowsill. "She went off to parties and balls, country houses and yachts. And she…left me…with strangers."

"Oh, Brandon…" Jana went to him, wanting nothing more than to throw her arms around him, comfort him. But Brandon pulled away, warding her off with his gaze, refusing to accept any kindness she offered.

"These people, were they good to you?"

"Most of them."

Jana forced herself to remain a short distance away. "Was she gone for long?"

"Weeks…months…" Brandon rubbed his forehead. "She'd take me to people she barely knew, reputable people from our social circle mostly, anybody who would agree to keep me. She'd say to them 'Just keep him until Sunday. I'll be back for him after services on Sunday.'"

"But she didn't come back?" Jana asked, her heart breaking as she spoke the words.

"Every Sunday I'd be as good as I possibly could in church. When we got back home I'd rush to the window and…wait." Brandon uttered a gruff laugh and tapped his knuckle against the glass pane in front of him.

"Sometimes I still catch myself standing at windows, looking out, waiting…for something."

"How did you end up with your grandfather in New York?" Jana asked. "Did he and your mother finally make amends?"

Brandon drew in a breath. "Actually, Leona Albright brought me home."

Her eyes widened. "Leona?"

"She was honeymooning in Europe with one of her husbands—I believe the fellow's name was Riley—and she happened to visit the home I was staying in. She was acquainted with the Delaney family in New York and knew the situation with my mother. When she realized who I was, and how I was being treated, she brought me home to my grandfather."

"It must have been a bit frightening for you," Jana said.

"I was ten years old, but I remember every moment of it," Brandon said, the tiniest smile tugging at his lips. "Onboard the ship during our return voyage, Leona played checkers with me. She read to me. She bought me ice cream. We walked the decks and spit off the railing together."

So that was the bond between the two of them. Jana understood it now. Leona had rescued him. Saved him. Cared for him. A debt so monstrous, Brandon could never repay it.

"Your grandfather must have been relieved to learn that you were all right," Jana said, "to have you safely under his roof."

"Some of the family deeply resented Leona for interfering. My appearance caused a bit of a scandal, as you can imagine, and stirred up all the old gossip about my mother's elopement years before."

"Did you like living with your grandfather?" she asked, easing a little closer to him.

"It was stable. After the way things turned out with my mother, Grandfather was less strict, less demanding with me, I'm told. He and I were never very close, but we tolerated each other." Brandon turned to the window again. "And sometimes on Sundays, I'd stand and look out, wondering if I'd see—"

He stopped, not saying anything more.

"Your mother." Jana finished the thought for him. "You'd look out the window, hoping to see her coming back for you."

Brandon turned away, not answering.

"Did you ever learn what happened to her?" Jana asked after a moment.

"Some years later, Grandfather received word that she'd died in France," Brandon said. He pushed on. "After I finished my education, Grandfather settled money on me and sent me here to California. It suited us both that I was out of the house. I don't think he expected much from me, given who my father was, and that pushed me to prove him wrong."

"Which you did," Jana said and gave him a prideful smile.

They fell silent then. Brandon's shoulders sagged a

little and he looked as if the things he'd told her had left him exhausted. And rightly so, Jana thought.

She understood now, for the first time, why he hadn't come after her in London. And the supreme sacrifice to his pride at asking her to come back to him.

Gently, she touched his arm. "Brandon, I'm so sorry. If I'd known how your mother abandoned you, I would never have run out on you like I did."

Another wave of emotion hit him and he waved his hand to silence her, but Jana couldn't stop.

"I'm sorry, Brandon. I'm so sorry," she said. "I wouldn't have complained about being home before six, either. That's the reason, isn't it? Because you don't want to be left standing, waiting. It's the reason you couldn't come after me in London, wasn't it?"

He managed a little nod. "All those painful memories of being left behind. Maybe it was pride, too. But I just couldn't bring myself to go after you, beg you to come home with me. I just…couldn't."

"I understand." Even though he didn't seem to want her to, Jana put her arms around him and laid her cheek against his chest. "I'm sorry, Brandon. I'm so sorry for hurting you."

He stood there for a while, letting her hold him, then stepped back. "I'm tired."

She didn't really want him to leave. She wished he'd sit with her on the settee, let everything he'd said sink in. Let her hold him and comfort him.

But Brandon wasn't ready for that. She wondered if he ever would be.

"Good night, then," Jana said.

When he left the room, she turned toward the window just as Brandon had done. Darkness had fallen. A few lights were visible in the distance.

So many things were clear in her mind now, where Brandon was concerned. His distance from his family. The peculiar relationship he shared with Leona Albright. His trouble displaying his emotions.

Her abandonment of him had been the worst, she realized. In taking her marriage vows, Jana had made a commitment to him, then ran away into the night without so much as a word. Just as his mother had done. Though a mother's commitment to her child remained the most important, Jana's own abandonment of Brandon must have hurt him nearly as much.

As with many men, Brandon derived much of his self-worth from his business success. This was especially true of Brandon's, where the family had expected little or nothing from him.

And she had just crippled his Jennings project. Yet another bad choice to heap on the mountain of others just like it.

Jana moved away from the window, too restless to sit, too tired to climb the stairs to her bedchamber.

After hearing about what his mother had done to him, how could she leave him? *Again?*

She couldn't. Jana knew in her heart that she couldn't walk out on Brandon another time. But it wasn't simply her guilty conscience that kept her here. She'd fallen in love with her husband all over again. She'd known it for a while now.

Yes, there was still a chance that Brandon would revert to his old ways, to the kind of behavior that had driven her away all those months ago. But after tonight, after his wrenching confession, she couldn't imagine that he wasn't sincere in his feelings for her.

She'd tell him everything. The idea sprang into Jana's head, bringing with it a surge of relief. She would explain about the baby, explain how she'd kept secrets from him, tell him why she'd chosen that course of action.

She'd stand up to his wrath, then ask him if they could stay together.

And if he didn't forgive her? Well, maybe she didn't deserve his forgiveness anyway.

Chapter Twenty-Five

A whole day later and Jana's decision to confess to Brandon everything she'd done still seemed like a good one.

Now, if she could only *tell* him.

Jana left her dressing room, pulling on her robe atop her pale blue nightgown. Abbie had already turned down the coverlet and vanished, leaving a lamp burning on her writing desk across the room.

All her good intentions had simmered since last night, waiting for the right time to tell Brandon. He'd left early this morning and hadn't come home yet this evening. He had sent word that he wouldn't be home until very late.

Jana could only imagine the problems he faced today. The collapse of his Jennings project, angry potential tenants, financial difficulties. While half the city, it seemed, hailed him as the champion for all womankind, the other half was angry with him for the position the *Messenger* had taken.

And as soon as he returned home tonight, Jana wanted to tell him that she'd had his baby and deliberately kept it a secret from him.

"Oh, lovely…"

Jana sat down on her vanity bench and stared at her reflection in the mirror. This evening was hardly the time to tell him. But would there ever be a *good* time for it?

More than anything she wanted to unburden herself of her misdeeds. All of them. Yet heaping them on Brandon after an already difficult day wouldn't be right.

She'd make an appointment with him. Jana plucked the pins from her hair and let it cascade down her back. Silly as it sounded, she would tell Brandon that she needed to speak with him and ask if he could come home early tomorrow evening. They could sit down together and she would tell him everything, explain herself.

And hope that he would forgive her.

Absently, Jana picked up her brush and ran it through her hair. Late this afternoon she'd run by the women's refuge and left articles and the Ask Mrs. Avery column in a sealed envelope for Oliver to pick up. With so much time on her hands today, Jana had written several, including "The Value of Good Manners," "Courtesy on the Street" and "The Etiquette of Stationery," enough to last for a number of issues of the *Messenger*. Answering the Mrs. Avery letters Oliver had given to her took a bit longer to compose. These were real women with real problems. She thought long and hard before addressing their concerns and giving her advice.

Her advice… Jana gave herself a sour look in the mirror and laid the brush aside. As if she'd done so well with her own life.

Aunt Maureen had been pleased with her decision, though, when Jana had stopped by the hotel and given her the news. Her aunt had always been fond of Brandon and was glad Jana was doing the right thing.

Aunt Maureen predicted Brandon would forgive her. But Jana wasn't so sure.

A soft knock sounded on the door and Jana waited, expecting Abbie to slip inside. She didn't, though, and when the knock came again, she answered the door.

Brandon waited outside, leaning against the door casing. Her heart picked up a little at the sight of him looking haggard and worn, but handsome as ever. His necktie was loosened and his collar open.

His gaze dipped, as always, taking her in from head to toe, then settled on her face. He drew in that long, languid breath she'd heard so often, the one that wordlessly spoke of his desire for her.

Suddenly Jana wanted to blurt out everything that was in her heart, everything she'd done and said, every mistake, every bad decision she'd made. More than anything, she wanted to hear Brandon say that he forgave her. That their marriage could be saved and they could be happy together.

But now was not the time. Here she stood wearing nothing but her gown and robe, her hair loose about her shoulders. If she confessed everything now, Brandon might think she'd dressed this way on purpose to distract him from what she was saying, to use her feminine wiles to gain favor.

No. Now was definitely not the time.

"I just wanted to let you know that I was home," Brandon said. His voice was low, his tone weary. "I...I didn't want you to think I'd stayed away because of yesterday."

"I didn't think that," she said. "I figured you had a tough day."

He nodded but didn't explain.

"Should I have Mrs. Boone bring you something to eat?" she offered.

Brandon shook his head as if he was too tired to eat. Another moment passed while he just looked at her. Finally, he turned away. "Good night."

"Brandon?"

He swung back around to face her, a hint of expectation in his gaze.

"I wondered if tomorrow you and I could set aside a time to talk?"

A look of complete despair came over him. "Just tell me now," he said, his voice flat, lifeless.

Jana gasped. He thought she intended to tell him she was leaving. What else would his reaction mean?

"This is hardly the time," she said quickly. "You've had a miserable day."

"Jana, please." He touched his fingers to his forehead. "I can't have this hanging over my head until tomorrow. Tell me."

"Well, all right," she said. "I'll dress quickly and we can go down to the sitting room—"

"There's no such thing as you dressing quickly." Brandon pushed past her into the bedchamber.

"But—"

"Say it, Jana. Whatever it is, just say it."

His expression told her that he wasn't sure where this was headed, but he feared the worst. Though these weren't the circumstances she imagined, Jana went ahead.

She pushed the door closed and faced him. "I've done a lot of thinking since I returned, and I've come to some decisions."

Brandon seemed to brace himself, not responding.

"I decided that you've worked very hard to change things about yourself," Jana said. "You've tried to understand why I left, and you've tried to make me happy here. I decided that your intentions seem genuine."

His brows drew together in a tight frown. "But…?"

"I decided that I don't want to wake up another morning and not find you beside me."

He stilled and tilted his head, as if not sure he trusted himself to believe what she'd said.

"You…you decided—what?"

"After I left you, Brandon, I thought our marriage didn't matter. If it was over, then perhaps that was for the best," Jana told him. "I thought I could live with my decision until I returned and saw you that first night. I knew in my heart that I still loved you."

He didn't move, made no effort to speak, so Jana continued.

"You've shown me that you can be different. I hope you've seen that I've changed too." Jana drew in a breath. "I've made a lot of mistakes, Brandon. I've made some very bad decisions. I want to tell you all of them, and ask for your forgiveness. And I hope that you'll still want me to stay with you and be your wife."

He started, her words finally sinking in, apparently.

"You mean—you'll stay?"

"Yes," she told him. "If you'll have me."

"And you won't leave me again?"

"No, Brandon. But you need to hear everything I have to tell you before—"

"We can live as man and wife again?"

"Yes, of course we can. But Brandon, I have other things to tell you. Important things that might influence your decision—"

"When?" He took a step toward her. "Tonight? *Now?*"

"Brandon, please listen to me," she pleaded. "You don't know what I've done. You might not want to forgive me—"

"I forgive you." Brandon yanked off his jacket.

"You can't forgive me," she insisted. "You don't even know what I've done."

"Whatever it is, I forgive you." He threw off his necktie and sent it flying across the room.

"I've done something. Something terrible," she told him.

He stood on one foot, tugged off his shoe and sock, then hopped on the other and did the same.

"Brandon, *please*!"

He strode forward and laid his hands on her shoulders. "If you don't want to make love tonight, I understand. It's been a long time and if you're not ready, it's fine."

"No, it's not that—"

"Thank God...." Brandon pulled her against him and buried his nose in her hair.

"Brandon, wait—"

"Ah, Jana, please don't ask me to wait. Please, I've waited so long already...."

She wiggled her arms between them and forced him away.

"I've done something terrible, Brandon. Something that you may decide is unforgivable. I want to tell you, explain it, before we—"

"I *know*." Brandon plucked open the buttons on his shirt and stripped it off. "Outside the hotel today I— never mind the details. I know everything."

She gasped, touched her fingers to her lips. "You do?"

"Yes." He dropped his suspenders.

How could he know? How could he possibly know? Unless he'd gone to the hotel today with the intention of seeing Aunt Maureen. She must have told him about the baby. How else could he have known?

"Oh, Brandon," she whispered.

"I forgive you."

"Are you sure?"

"Hell, yes."

"But I feel I should explain——"

"I don't need an explanation," he told her.

"I want to explain," she insisted.

He caught her shoulder again, this time looking hard at her face. "What's done is done, Jana. We can't go back in time and change it. So let's *go forward*."

"Do you really mean that, Brandon?"

He tensed, his eyes widening, his breath puffing hotter and faster. "If you don't want to make love now, please just say so."

She smiled, relieved beyond belief that he'd forgiven her. It was a dream come true. They would speak of it later, talk through the details. She'd feel better once she'd told him everything that was in her heart.

But right now, Brandon wanted no part of talking. Raw desire seeped from him. It covered Jana, wound through her, flamed fires left dormant for too long.

"I want us to make love tonight," she said softly.

He held back. "You're sure you're ready?"

"I'm ready," she told him and gave him a saucy smile. "Are you?"

Brandon eased a little closer. "I've been ready every day of the last fourteen months."

"Then maybe we should get on with it?"

He moaned deep in his throat and pulled her full against him. She shifted her hips over him; he was ready, all right.

Brandon pushed her hair over her shoulder and laid

his mouth against her neck. A shiver passed through her and she leaned her head sideways, allowing him to do as he chose.

Joy rose inside her because this time she didn't have to hold back or spurn his advances. She was free to enjoy him.

His lips took hers in a deep kiss. Jana moaned as his tongue slid inside, finding familiar places. He opened the buttons of her robe and pushed it off her shoulders. It pooled at her feet. Jana's arms circled his neck as she returned his exquisite kiss.

His fingers fumbled with the front buttons of her nightgown. She felt the fabric part to just above her waist and his hands move inside to capture both her breasts.

She gasped. Brandon groaned. He worked his most delightful magic on her, kneading, cupping. Then he bent low and kissed a hot trail down so that his mouth took over from his hands.

Jana ran her palms over the fabric of his white cotton undershirt, stretched tight over his hard chest. When his lips claimed her mouth again, she slid her fingers downward and popped open the buttons on his trousers. They fell to the floor and he stepped out of them. She touched him. Her palm burned from the heat he gave off, despite the flannel underdrawers that separated them.

Brandon groaned deep in his throat and swept her into his arms. He placed her on the bed and stretched out beside her.

His kisses deepened, became hotter, more demanding. He eased her nightgown off her shoulders. His hands, his mouth found her breasts over and over. Jana lost herself in his attention. She'd missed him. She'd missed their lovemaking. He knew what she liked, where to touch, how to please.

She knew how to please him as well. The sensitive spots, the private places. Things a husband and wife knew about each other.

Yet she knew those things would come later. Tomorrow morning, or tomorrow afternoon. Tonight, Brandon was in a hurry.

It had been too long for both of them. Jana shifted as he bunched her nightgown around her hips. He fumbled with his drawers and climbed between her thighs. She welcomed the weight of his body atop hers.

Jana looked at him in the dim light. Bulging arm muscles. Wide, straight shoulders. The tenseness in his face that resulted from sheer delight.

He eased forward, touching himself against her. Jana squeezed her knees against his sides, stilling him.

She stroked her fingers through his hair and gazed into his questioning eyes.

"This is what I liked about us," she whispered. "This moment. Just you and me. No business deals. No appointments. No one else. This is what I liked about us."

"Ah, Jana…I love you so much."

"I love you…oh…"

He eased inside her, then stopped. It had been a long

time. He curled his fists into the pillow beneath her head, struggling to hold back. Slowly he moved, finally making a place for himself.

Jana caught his rhythm. It built quickly. Her hips arched, meeting his. Then those waves of pleasure that Brandon provided so effortlessly broke through her again and again. She grabbed his hair and called his name. He wrapped her in both arms, buried his face against her neck, and followed.

Another morning waking with Brandon sharing her bed.

A little smile pulled at Jana's lips as her eyes fluttered open to the faint light of dawn streaming in through the window. For so long she'd thought she never wanted this moment to happen again. Now it had, and she couldn't be happier.

Brandon would surely be as happy, as soon as he woke up. He lay beside her, his arm draped across her, one leg atop hers. No doubt about what had gone on in this bed last night. Her nightgown was unfastened to her waist, still gathered up around her hips. Brandon wore his undershirt. His drawers had worked down a little ways.

He stirred, his head on the pillow close to hers. When he opened his eyes, she smiled. He smiled too and pushed himself up. A stubble of dark whiskers covered his jaw. His hair stuck out on one side.

"Good morning," she said quietly, smoothing the errant shock of hair into place.

He leaned down and planted a soft kiss on her lips. "That's the best night's sleep I've had in months."

She smiled. "Me, too."

"Ask me," he said, grinning.

"Ask you what?"

"What you used to always ask," he said. "Ask me to stay home with you today."

A giddy laugh slipped out. "You'd do that? You'd stay with me?"

He gave her an apologetic half smile. "Things were a little different last night. A little rushed."

"We're out of practice."

Brandon lifted her hand and pressed it to his lips. "We could stay here together today, if you'd like? Get to know each other again."

"Practice makes perfect."

That knowing grin she hadn't seen in so long came back.

"Can I look at you?" he asked. "All of you? In the light?"

She hesitated. "You might not like what you see."

"I doubt that…." Brandon got to his knees, caught her gown and pulled it over her head. "You're just as beautiful as I remember—"

He froze. Didn't move an inch. Didn't draw a breath. Confusion drew his features tight.

Jana spread her hand across her lower abdomen, splaying her fingers to hide the marks childbirth had left on her. They weren't pretty. She knew that.

Horror overcame Brandon's face. "You've—you've had a *baby*."

She blinked up at him. "Well, yes—"

"You've had a baby!" Brandon bounded off the bed, faced her with uncontrolled fury. "While you were in London! You had a baby—didn't you!"

Jana sat up, not understanding. "You said you knew. Last night, you said you'd found out yesterday. That it didn't matter. You said—"

"What the hell are you talking about?" He roared the words, sounding like a animal wounded beyond comprehension.

"Outside the Morgan Hotel," Jana said, frantic now to make him remember. "You said you were there and found out—"

"That you were Mrs. Avery! I saw Fisk and he told me you were behind that Mrs. Avery column!"

"Oh, Brandon—"

"Whose is it?" he asked, his voice now low and guttural. He pointed at her belly, his hand shaking. "Whose baby did you have?"

She gasped. Her hand went to her throat. He thought she'd had someone else's baby? Is that what he meant? Could that possibly be what he thought?

"Who was it! Some man you took up with on the ship! Someone you stumbled across in London!" He drew in a hot, ragged breath. "Get out of my house. I want you gone before I come home tonight. And don't you ever come back again."

He stormed out of the room, slamming the door so hard the window shook.

Jana broke into tears.

Chapter Twenty-Six

Nothing had ever hurt like this before. Two broken fingers. A horse kick. A fight that sent him through a glass window. Nothing had caused this much pain.

Not even when she left the first time.

Brandon shoved his hands into his trouser pockets and plodded on. He'd walked the city all day. Wandered aimless through the streets since he'd headed for his office this morning, then bypassed the building without going inside. Nothing that awaited mattered to him.

Nothing mattered.

For most of the day he hadn't been able to comprehend what had happened. Hearing last night that Jana would stay with him. Making sweet love to her. Then waking to find himself caught in the ultimate betrayal.

Brandon turned a corner, not sure what part of town he was in now. Not caring, either.

Should he have known what Jana had done? Should he have seen it? The signs were there. Her calm demeanor. The patience she showed. Her fuller breasts and more mature figure. Her choice of clothing that made her look like a grown woman, rather than a mere girl. Their lovemaking last night had been different. Had he just refused to put the clues together, see what was right in front of his eyes?

He didn't know. Hell, he didn't know anything right now.

Except that he'd never been more miserable in his life.

For a moment he toyed with the idea of going to Leona Albright. But he dismissed the thought. She couldn't give him ice cream and spit off the railing and make *this* better for him.

The hurt was too deep. It would never go away. Betrayed by his wife, the one person he truly loved.

Why had she done it? If he knew, maybe he could understand.

Brandon looked up, tried to get his bearings, then headed for the Morgan Hotel. Her aunt could explain what had happened. He quickened his pace. Yes, he'd ask her aunt.

At the registration desk, Brandon asked for the room number. The young man who'd been on duty the last time he was there didn't bother to check the records.

"I'm sorry, sir, but Miss Armstrong and her party checked out," he said. "This morning."

The words hit Brandon like a kick in the gut. He turned away.

Oh, God. She was really gone.

Home.

But only because there was no place else to go.

"Have my things packed," Brandon said to Charles as he stepped into the foyer.

"But, sir—"

"I'm staying at a hotel for a while." He passed the butler his bowler and walked slowly away.

Everything he looked at reminded him of Jana. The construction still not finished. The wallpaper sample books. The breakfast room, the garden, that tiny little storage room she'd shoved him in, calling it his study.

He didn't know how he'd bear going upstairs.

All he knew was that he couldn't stay in this house any longer. He'd sell it, furniture and all. Maybe he'd leave the city, the state…the country.

Her scent still permeated the place, as vibrant as if she still lived here. Brandon headed down the hallway for one last look at the sitting room she loved so much. He stepped inside and—

There she sat.

Jana looked up from the book on her lap and saw Brandon in the doorway. She couldn't read the expression on his face. Stunned at seeing her, yes. But furious? Or thrilled? She couldn't be sure.

"What the hell are you doing here?"

Not furious. Angry, though. She could accept that.

Jana placed her book aside. "I'm not going anywhere," she told him.

"I told you this morning I wanted you gone, that I never wanted to see you again," he said through clenched teeth.

So much was at stake here, yet Jana had never experienced such a calm in her life.

She gazed steadily at him. "I'm not leaving. I am never going to leave you again, Brandon. I won't abandon you, or desert you, or walk out on you. If you want me gone, you'll have to pick me up and dump me on the street yourself."

He glared at her, so much hurt in his eyes. But she could make it go away. If he'd let her.

"Just remember," Jana said. "If you throw me out, you'll be losing two of us."

His brows drew together. "What is that supposed to mean?"

She gestured across the room to a white bassinet sitting in the corner.

"Your son."

Brandon's gaze darted to the bassinet, then to her again. He pulled back a little.

"Mine?" he asked, almost in a whisper.

"Yes, yours. Never mind that you accused me of adultery, plus a few other ugly things while I was in London. We'll get to those another day. Right now, I'd like you to meet your son."

"You were—before you left here, you were carrying my child?"

"I didn't know it, but yes, I was," she said. "I realized it only after I'd arrived in London. I thought I was seasick."

He looked angry again. "Then why didn't you come back right away?"

"Because you weren't exactly my favorite person at that time," Jana told him. "But mostly, it was because I refused to risk the crossing."

His glare turned more menacing. "You kept him from me."

She rose from the chair. No reason to hold back now. "You were a terrible husband. I decided you'd make an even worse father. I wouldn't subject my child to that sort of life. So, yes, I kept him a secret. I intended to secure a divorce and never tell you about him.

"Of course," she went on, "you spoiled my plans by turning out to be a wonderful husband. I have no doubt you'll make a wonderful father. If you want us, that is."

Once more, Brandon's gaze jumped to the bassinet for a moment. "Show me some proof. A doctor's notice, a birth registry. Something that gives his birth date."

"No."

His jaw tightened. "No?"

"No," she said again. "You have to accept us in your heart, Brandon. Both of us. If you can't do that then there's no point in us staying."

He didn't answer, didn't move, just stared at her.

"He looks like you," Jana said, then gave him a wry smile. "Unfortunately, he's inherited my disposition."

Jana went to Brandon and slid her arm through his. "Come meet your son."

He didn't budge. For a long moment he simply looked down at her. Then, finally, Jana led him across the room.

The baby lay sleeping on his back in the bassinet, his hands curled into fists, a shock of light brown hair covering his crown.

"Your son," Jana said, gesturing. "Nicholas Brandon Sayer."

"You named him after me?"

"And my father. I hope you don't mind."

"He's so big." Brandon glanced at her belly. "He was actually inside you?"

"He's been growing for a while now."

A long moment passed while they stood side by side, looking down at the baby.

"He's really mine?" Brandon asked, as if perhaps he was afraid to believe it.

"Yes."

"Do you have a birth registry?"

"Do I need one?"

Brandon shook his head. "No."

"I'm so sorry for all the hurt I caused you." Jana stretched up and kissed his cheek. "Ready to hold your son now?"

"Hold him? I've never held a baby before, and I—"

"Wake up, sleepyhead, and meet your papa." Jana lifted the baby from the bassinet. He fussed and gurgled, then burst out crying.

"See? I told you he had my disposition," Jana said and laid him in Brandon's arms.

"Wait, Jana, no," he said, juggling the baby awkwardly. "He's crying."

"You'll get used to it."

Brandon held the baby away from him. "Something's wet under here."

"Consider yourself christened."

"But—"

"Relax, Brandon, you'll be fine." Jana eased the baby against Brandon's chest, then slid her arms around the two of them. "We'll all be fine. As long as we're together."

"Excuse me, Mrs. Sayer."

Jana turned her attention to the doorway of the sitting room and saw Charles.

"Yes?"

"Mr. Sayer has arrived home."

"Already?" She glanced at the mantel clock. "It isn't even noon yet. Where is he? Never mind. I know."

"Yes, ma'am," Charles said and nodded wisely.

Jana climbed the stairs to the second floor, knowing without a doubt where to find Brandon. After spending three full days at home together, she'd learned his habits very well.

If he wasn't in bed with her, he was in the nursery with the baby.

At the end of the hallway, that's exactly where she found him. He'd already run off the nanny and was sitting in the rocking chair, little Nicholas sleeping in his arms.

Tears of joy pooled in Jana's eyes. Big, sturdy, strong Brandon, cradling his fragile son with such care. Her heart ached with happiness.

"A half day at the office was all you could stand?" she asked, sniffing back her tears.

"I handled everything," he said, keeping his voice down so as not to wake the baby. "Well, everything that absolutely couldn't wait."

"What about your Jennings project?"

He tilted his head. "You did an outstanding job of sabotaging several months of work. You cost me a small fortune and, very nearly, my best friend."

She cringed. "I'm sorry."

"Not to worry," Brandon said. "I've put the pieces back together again, though it did cost me yet another small fortune."

"Sorry," she said again, giving him a weak smile. "What did you do?"

"Bought another building to house the *Messenger*. We're going ahead with the renovations for the Jennings building, honoring the leases. Everyone is pleased."

"Including Noah?"

"Including Noah," Brandon said.

"What about your other friends?" Jana asked. "Are they still upset with you over the articles in the newspaper?"

"Things are calming down. I guess a little controversy isn't such a bad thing," Brandon said. "Although, it would be a good idea to keep your Mrs. Avery identity a secret."

"I agree," Jana said. "I went by the women's refuge first thing this morning to check on the volunteer list. Oliver was there. Have you seen him lately? He seems more self-confident, more self-assured. Do you think the success of the newspaper brought this on?"

Brandon thought a few "afternoon teas" with Leona had brought it on, but didn't say so.

"Oliver asked Noah if he could call on Audrey," Brandon said. "He said yes, naturally."

"Oh, that's wonderful. Oliver and Audrey make such a nice couple, don't you think?"

"I think you and I make a nice couple," Brandon told her, grinning. He rose from the rocker, steadying the baby so as not to wake him. "I was thinking, though, that we might try something more to cement our marriage."

Jana walked over. "Other than trying to have another baby? And you are working awfully hard at it, Brandon, giving it your very best effort."

"You have my tireless, unceasing devotion to the cause," he told her. "But I was thinking that with the renovations to the Jennings building underway, and since I've fired that decorator, what's-his-name, that you could pick out the paint and wallpaper and things."

"I'd like that," Jana said. "I guess you noticed your study downstairs. I hope you don't mind that I changed the color again."

"Dark blue, walnut furniture, hunting scenes on the walls." Brandon pulled his brows together. "It's not lilac, but I guess I'll learn to live with it."

Jana slid her arm through his and snuggled close. "I got a telegram from Aunt Maureen this morning. She's safely back in San Francisco, and wishes us well."

Brandon leaned down and kissed her gently on the lips.

"I love you," he whispered.

"I love you, too," she answered. "Do you know what I like about us?"

"The lovemaking?" he asked, wiggling his eyebrows playfully.

"Well, yes," she admitted. "But there's something else."

Jana curled one arm around Brandon's shoulder and stroked her fingers through the baby's soft hair.

"What I like about us," she said, "is that now there're three of us."

* * * * *

FALL IN LOVE WITH
THESE HANDSOME HEROES
FROM HARLEQUIN HISTORICALS

On sale September 2004

THE PROPOSITION
by Kate Bridges

Sergeant Major Travis Reid
Honorable Mountie of the Northwest

WHIRLWIND WEDDING
by Debra Cowan

Jericho Blue
Texas Ranger out for outlaws

On sale October 2004

ONE STARRY CHRISTMAS
by Carolyn Davidson/Carol Finch/Carolyn Banning

Three heart-stopping heroes
for your Christmas stocking!

THE ONE MONTH MARRIAGE
by Judith Stacy

Brandon Sayer
Businessman with a mission

www.eHarlequin.com
HARLEQUIN HISTORICALS®

HHWEST33

Savor the breathtaking
romances and thrilling adventures
of Harlequin Historicals

On sale September 2004

THE KNIGHT'S REDEMPTION by Joanne Rock

A young Welshwoman tricks Roarke Barret into marriage
in order to break her family's curse—of spinsterhood.
But Ariana Glamorgan never expects to fall for the
handsome Englishman who is now her husband....

PRINCESS OF FORTUNE by Miranda Jarrett

Captain Lord Thomas Greaves is assigned to guard Italian
princess Isabella di Fortunaro. Sparks fly and passions flare
between the battle-weary captain and the spoiled, beautiful
lady. Can love cross all boundaries?

On sale October 2004

HIGHLAND ROGUE by Deborah Hale

To save her sister from a fortune hunter, Claire Talbot offers
herself as a more tempting target. But can she forget the
feelings she once had for Ewan Geddes, a charming
Highlander who once worked on her father's estate?

THE PENNILESS BRIDE by Nicola Cornick

Home from the Peninsula War, Rob Selbourne discovers
he must marry a chimney sweep's daughter to
fulfill his grandfather's eccentric will. Will Rob
find true happiness in the arms of
the lovely Jemima?

www.eHarlequin.com

HARLEQUIN HISTORICALS®